Can't Choose Your Family

Patsy Collins

To my sister-in-law Cindy.
Because you're one of us.

Contents

1. Can't Choose Your Family

It's sad to say, the first thing I thought when I saw my son's shiny new car pull up outside was, "Wonder what he wants now?"

That probably sums Doug up. He's not really bad, but he does tend to put himself before anyone else. Take the business with the dog for instance. My grandson Luke had wanted one. Really, really, wanted one, and had done for some time. Doug must have known that; it had been on the lad's letter to Santa and if he saw a dog anywhere he always asked if he could stroke it. His favourite toy was a stuffed dog and he had pictures of dogs on his bedroom wall.

When Doug had asked Luke what he'd like for his birthday of course a dog was what he'd asked for. Doug had refused outright and said he'd buy a train set.

"We can play with that together," he told me when I queried that choice.

"You could walk a dog together."

"Don't you start, Dad. Luke's not old enough to look after it properly so it'd be down to Gracie. She's got enough to do without having to deal with dog hairs on the furniture and my suits, plus there's the expense."

I'd been rather pleased he spared a thought for his wife in amongst that, even though I suspected mostly he was concerned she'd have less time to fuss over him.

"Since Luke suggested it I've been thinking I'd rather like to have a dog myself," I told him. That was perfectly true, although my main motives were Luke's happiness and the chance to see the lad more often. "We could get a rescue one between us and keep it at my place. It won't cost you anything and Luke can walk it and groom it anytime he likes."

"I suppose so."

Luke had been thrilled when his parents and I broke the news.

"What colour will he be? What will we call him? Can we go and get one now?"

Even Doug smiled at that.

"Not just yet," I said. "We need to pick out the right one and the people who look after dogs which are waiting for new homes will have to come and check we have a good place for him to live."

"My bed is comfy, Grandad. The dog will like it."

"He's going to sleep at Grandad's house, remember?" Gracie said.

"Does that mean he'll be Grandad's dog and not mine?"

"He'll be our dog, yours, mine Daddy's and Grandad's, isn't that right?" she asked me.

I agreed with her and it seemed as though we had the perfect arrangement. I'd have the companionship of the dog all the time and would see even more of my family too.

We'd gone to the rescue home and met lots of dogs. One was just perfect for us. About three years old and housetrained, small and friendly but with plenty of energy to play all day with a six-year-old and his grandfather. It wasn't the prettiest of things due to having a few bald patches, but as it had a great deal more hair than I did I wasn't in a position to mind that. We'd arranged a date for someone to come round to do the necessary checks at my place.

"Hi, Dad, only me," Doug called as he let himself in a few days later. He sounded a bit subdued somehow.

I was in the kitchen making a pot of tea. Doug often says he doesn't have time if I offer to make one, but if the kettle has already boiled he'll usually stay long enough to drink a cup.

Had Doug come to say he'd changed his mind about sharing his family's affection with a four-legged friend? I wasn't going to give in easily if that was the case and got ready to say I wasn't going to let him disappoint the rest of us.

The news was worse than that. He and Gracie were splitting up. Doug had been having an affair for a few months and Gracie had found out. I just couldn't understand it. I'd been devastated to lose my own wife. How could my son do such a thing voluntarily? As he talked on I tried to make sense of it. Doug didn't even seem to love the new woman. He just talked about her looks and how she wasn't always too busy with a son to take notice of him. There was nothing about the woman's personality or regret for the pain he was causing.

Eventually my reaction seemed to make an impression. "You don't seem very supportive, Dad. I'm the one being kicked out but you're not interested in how I feel."

"No, I'm not! I can't believe my son could be so selfish."

"Yeah, well I'm not your son am I?"

That was the first time in years he'd said such a thing. I am 'only' his stepdad but I'd brought him up as mine since he was a toddler and I'm the only father he's ever known. During a difficult patch in his teens he'd occasionally yelled, "You're not my real dad." I'd put that down to hormones. I'd never yelled back, but for the first time I wanted to.

"Luke is your son though isn't he? Have you thought about him?"

"I'll still see him sometimes."

"A part-time father to go with the part-time dog?"

"What? You can't still get the dog."

"Why on earth not?"

"Hardly loyal is it? Besides, from the way Gracie reacted I doubt she'll want anything to do with you."

It seems Doug had told his wife he'd been with me on several occasions when really he'd been with the other woman. She'd likely think I'd been covering up for him and maybe she'd blame me for bringing him up to be selfish. Truth be told, because of the stepdad thing I had spoiled him a bit, let him have his own way too often. Maybe a share of the blame did lie with me.

I'd understand it if she wasn't keen on seeing me but loyalty was another matter. I'd promised Luke and his mother that I'd care for the dog and wanted to keep that promise. Luke might be allowed to visit sometimes and besides there was the animal to consider. Sharing it with Luke had been my main motivation, but I'd need companionship more than ever now and I could still offer a decent home to a dog which needed one.

Every day I went and took him on a good long walk and

got to know him properly. He was really excitable around other dogs and people, meaning I had to keep him on a lead most of the time to stop him diving in where he wasn't wanted. It was just over-friendliness, but of course some people don't want a dog launching himself at them however pleasant his intentions. Other than that, he was no trouble. If we went somewhere quiet he'd race about off the lead and come back when called. He'd sit on command and leave his ball or a chew when told to do so.

I took to calling him Dawg. It didn't seem right to give him a proper name as I'd promised Luke he could decide and the animal seemed happy to answer to anything. The home visit was fine and a day arranged for me to pick him up.

As the staff waved me and Dawg off, one of them made a comment about hoping he'd be happy with his new dad. That's probably what got me thinking about Gracie. She must have known my true relationship to Doug but never mentioned it. She'd accepted me as Luke's grandad. Maybe she still would? I should give us all that chance, besides I wanted to let Luke know I had the dog.

First though I took Dawg for a walk. If I drove him straight over there he'd be uncontrollable with excitement when we arrived. An hour of fetch left him happy to lie quietly in the car and stay there when I pulled up outside the house.

I'd not even locked my door when I heard Luke yell, "Grandad!" He came running at such a speed I quickly let myself in through the front gate for fear he'd run out into the street. Gracie was following more slowly but I knew that what might seem an impertinence on my part would be a lot more forgivable than any risk to Luke's safety.

I bent down and hugged the lad. "It's good to see you."

"Are you still my grandad? Dad says you aren't."

"It's not up to your dad now, lad. It's your mother you need to ask."

I looked up, hoping so hard it hurt that she'd give a nod to say she'd allow me a place in her son's life, but she'd walked right by me.

Dawg had started yapping and she was looking in at him. He stood up on his back legs and stuck his nose through the gap I'd left in the window and was trying to stretch his tongue out far enough to lick her.

"Is that our dog?" Gracie asked.

"Is he, Grandad? Is he?"

"Of course he is. I picked him up today and am taking him home to live, but you can come round and walk him and play with him anytime you like. Well, anytime your mum says it's OK."

"Can I walk him now? What's his name? Does he chase balls? Can I stroke him? Can we let him out to play in the garden?"

Gracie and I shared a grin over his enthusiasm and the way the dog was mirroring it from behind the glass.

"He does chase balls, yes. I don't know his name yet because you haven't told me and he's always ready to play, but… " I couldn't think of a way to explain I'd have to take Dawg away and Luke would have to wait until he visited me.

"Why don't we all walk him now?" Gracie suggested.

"Good idea," I agreed.

"Go and put your boots and coat on then, Luke." When he ran to obey, Gracie turned to me. "When we get the pair of them calmed down perhaps you'd like to bring him in for a while and we can all think of a name?"

"I'd like that, but… " as I clipped on the lead I indicated the hairy mess in the back of my car.

"Dog hairs are the least of my problems. I can vacuum them up and I'm starting to think maybe the others will sort themselves out in time."

"If there's anything I can do to help?"

"You've already started, you and this latest addition to our family."

2. Get Me To The Church On Time

So much for looking fantastic at my cousin's wedding. I'd planned to spend the morning showering, waxing, curling and painting. I'd arrive in time to impress my family before the blushing bride pushed me back into the shadows. Now I'll be lucky to get there before they've said 'I do'. There certainly won't be time for the full beauty treatment beforehand.

For once, I won't mind being in Vickie's shadow; the bride should be the centre of attention. I'd just have liked to have looked good myself too. Vickie and I never got on as children, although our families pretended we did and threw us together as much as possible. Whenever we had a row, it was always me who was caught shouting, throwing things, or pulling hair. Vickie did those things too, but was always apparently innocent in front of witnesses.

She was the adventurous one. I was the one who messed up. Vickie represented her school at athletics; I sprained my ankle playing hockey. Once she dared me to dye my hair. Vickie's hair had subtle lowlights; mine went the colour of orange squash.

Vickie sailed through her exams without the need for revision. Whilst she was going on dates, I was at home swotting, to achieve grades not quite as good as hers. Vickie got a job as a lawyer's assistant; I began training as a researcher for local radio. We kept out of each other's way, until I was asked to get some background on her boss, ready for his interview on a news feature. We'd met in a wine bar and both tried to be icily professional. We burst out laughing at exactly the same moment.

"Sorry, Sal," she said. "I noticed you've had your hair done and couldn't help remembering when I tricked you into making you turn it orange. D'you remember?"

"I remember the result, I hadn't realised you'd planned that. Still I suppose you had good reason after what I'd done to your face."

"What did you do? Not that rash thing?"

"Yeah, sorry."

"But how?"

"Every time you nodded off whilst sunbathing, I dabbed some self-tanning lotion on you. Then when your mum gave you that ointment, I switched that for lotion too."

"Oooh, clever. Bitchy, but clever."

We ordered another glass of wine and compared notes on the pranks we'd played. She confessed to the laxative chocolate she'd fed me and I admitted reprogramming her phone so her boyfriends' numbers were listed under each other's names. By the time we'd decided the score was even we'd also finished the bottle and called a truce. We've been friends since and I don't want to be late for her wedding

I shouldn't be at work today, but someone is off sick. Someone higher up the pecking order than me, so being asked to stand in for her is a big step.

"Just for a couple of hours, Sally. I'd really appreciate it," the producer had coaxed.

I'd showered, grabbed my vanity case and collected my dress from the dry cleaners on the way in. There wouldn't be time to do my legs or attempt anything fancy with my hair, but I'd be able to make myself presentable and arrive on time. Getting ready at work would save me driving home, then back past the studio onto the motorway.

Well, that's what I thought until I arrived. I was informed the two hours I was to work had become three and a half. I could have walked out the studio when they told me, but the look on the producer's face said it'd be a mistake.

My dream is to have a show of my own; there is no chance of ever achieving that unless I prove myself to be reliable and flexible. I can't let my boss down and I can't let Vickie down. I have to think of something fast.

Suddenly it occurs to me, I work for a radio station; it doesn't matter what I look like as long as I do my job. Every time I play a song, I get out my make-up and heated tongs and set to work. For a time half my hair is beautifully straightened and the rest a damp frizz. I get some funny looks as I dash to the coffee machine with immaculate make-up, superb hair and my usual scruffy jeans.

I check my printed directions. If I leave the moment we go off air and drive as fast as legally permitted, I'll just arrive on time. That is assuming the road is perfectly clear, not likely on a Saturday morning.

I've just slipped into my dress as the traffic report jingle airs.

"The A4 is completely blocked northbound just after junction 4. Thanks to Volvo Vixen for calling that one in." An alternative route is suggested.

Great, everyone will be on the other road; traffic will be backed up for miles, all because of someone's silly mistake. The exact same thing happened last week.

The moment the programme finishes I sprint out the door. I don't even stop for my discarded clothes and make-up kit. The traffic on the recommended alternate route is almost stationary.

It isn't until after the speeches and the cutting of the cake that Vickie has the chance to speak to me. I notice she wisely hadn't used the 'special' soap I sent for her big day. Maybe she didn't want the 'something blue' to be her skin.

"I was listening to your traffic report whilst I was having my facial, Sal. I heard all about the traffic chaos, how on earth did you get here on time?"

"The funny thing is, when I got to the A4 it was perfectly clear. I sometimes think the people who call the show just make up their information," I say, before I sneak out.

I'm going to 'decorate' the new Volvo that Mr and Mrs Fox will be going away in, just in case Vickie needs reminding that there's more than one vixen in this family.

3. Too Many Cooks?

Everything had been going really well until my fiancé, Kenny, got the phone call. Kenny, his daughter Stacey, and I had been enjoying a weekend together. We'd all gone to the pictures and then to a burger bar for tea.

I'd usually avoided getting involved in such outings as I thought Stacey needed some time alone with her dad. Now Kenny and I are living together and have a wedding date set, I too needed to spend some time with his daughter. I'd worked that out as soon as we'd told her about the wedding. It hadn't gone well.

"She hates me," I'd told my mum over the phone while Kenny drove Stacey home the previous week.

"Oh dear, Hannah. Dear little Stacey didn't like hearing about your wedding?" Mum asked.

"Actually, she was OK then and asked if I was going to have a dress like a princess. She looked at a bridal magazine and although I got the impression she thinks my dress sense is a bit plain, she seemed happy. It was when I made tea that we fell out."

"You can't mean she doesn't like your cooking?"

"No, she loves it nearly as much as Kenny does. I decided to make a special chocolate cheesecake to celebrate and I was just decorating it when Stacey came in wanting to help. Like an idiot I let her and she completely ruined it."

"Ruined it, or just didn't decorate it as neatly as you would have done? You can be something of a perfectionist."

"Mum! You sound just like Kenny. I apologised for the way it looked but he said it looked beautiful because he knew she was the one who'd daubed great dollops of chocolate sauce all over it."

"It probably did look beautiful to him."

"Yes, because she did it. If I'd done it, he'd have seen it was a mess. I told him that and we had a row. I overreacted, didn't I?"

"It sounds like it, love."

"It's just that I try so hard to get everything right, but I know that whatever I do, he'll always love her more. I'm not going to let a seven-year-old girl get between me and the man I'm marrying."

"Of course you shouldn't, but it doesn't have to be like that, I hope. Naturally he loves her, but that doesn't mean he cares any less for you. Remember that it's difficult for her too. You probably hurt her feelings when she was trying to help you."

I remember the look on the poor kid's face when I told her it would have been better if she hadn't interfered.

"I suppose I did, Mum. Actually, I know I did. I don't know how to put things right. I've got no experience of these things. No, that's no excuse is it? You were a single child too and you've always been a brilliant mum to me."

"You don't need to be a mum to Stacey," she advised me. "She's got one already. I don't know if she's brilliant or not, but she is Stacey's mum and you can't compete with that."

"So I might as well give up now?"

"Not at all. You can be a wonderful stepmum instead. Be a friend to her. You didn't have brothers or sisters but you had plenty of friends. Can't you think of something you used to like doing?"

So on the Saturday the three of us had gone to see a cartoon at the cinema. Instead of fussing that Stacey was wrapped up warmly and ate a proper meal, I left that to Kenny and helped Stacey chose and eat the best pick 'n' mix and later to construct the toy from her Happy Meal. It was a glittery plastic necklace and tiara.

When we got home, I let Stacey wear my shiny sandals and I braided her hair, threading ribbons through it. I even let her try on one of my dresses. She did look sweet and we both giggled a lot.

Later, Stacey had wanted to play Scrabble. I ganged up with her against Kenny. I 'secretly' helped her with her spelling and she pointed out the double letter squares for me to use. If our maths was correct, she and I tied for first place. We danced a victory dance around Kenny. Stacey asked for me to tuck her in.

"What are we doing tomorrow, Hannah?" she asked me.

"It's a secret, but it's something fun," I promised.

Kenny got the phone call just after breakfast and just before we'd told Hannah we were taking her to the zoo.

"Girls, I'm really sorry, but I've got to go into work for a while."

As I said, it had all been going really well up until then. Kenny would need to take the car, so I couldn't take Stacey to the zoo. I was glad we hadn't mentioned that, so she was spared the disappointment, but I was still stuck alone with a child whom I'd promised a day of fun.

"You'll be OK, won't you?" Kenny asked.

What could I say? Luckily Stacey answered.

"Course we will, Daddy. Hannah and I will have fun, she

promised."

I considered locking myself in the loo and phoning my mum for help. That probably wouldn't have helped though, hadn't she already said that I shouldn't act like a mum to Stacey? I was to be more like an older friend; just like my mum's oldest friend Aunty Betty had been to me when I was a kid. She'd been nothing like a parent; she'd spoilt me rotten and taken me on amazing adventures. That didn't help either.

Kenny and I had agreed with Stacey's mum that'd we'd all be consistent with our rules and never get into a situation where we tried to buy her affection or allowed her to play one parent against the other. I'd seen this was fair and best for Stacey as well as her mum, so simply buying Stacey lots of treats to keep her quiet until Kenny came back was out of the question. An amazing adventure seemed impossible without a car too.

"What did work say?" I asked Kenny, stalling for time.

"Just, 'Kenny, the lights won't work'."

He's the electrician, so clearly he had to go in. The words reminded me of something Aunty Betty used to say. 'Many hands make light work,' she said whenever I'd wanted to help her cook. She's a fabulous cook and an excellent teacher and it was from her I gained my culinary skill and love of good food.

I've long since realised that as a toddler I can't have been nearly so much help as I'd thought at the time. After the earlier experience with Stacey, I understood I must have been a real nuisance, yet somehow Aunty Betty still managed to serve up delicious meals. Maybe I could still learn something from Betty?

"Quick, Stacey, coat on. Kenny, can you drop us in town on your way?"

"Yes, but why?" he asked.

"It's a secret," I told him and winked at Stacey.

"I know, I know," Stacey said. "It's something fun, isn't it, Hannah?"

"Sure is."

The first part of our amazing adventure was a trip to the supermarket. Not so exciting for a grown woman, but a real novelty to a seven-year-old who is choosing what to buy for a special meal she's going to help make for her daddy.

"We're making it, you and me?" Stacey asked.

"Yes, Stacey. It's going to be very special, much too special for me to make all by myself."

The three course lunch was an absolute triumph. We had prawn cocktail for starters, garnished with cucumber that Stacey had cut into very interesting shapes. The entrée was a toasted cheese sandwich. For dessert we had rice crispy cakes. These were decorated with cherries, marshmallows and icing in three vivid colours. Very classy.

"That was fantastic," Kenny declared.

"You could have food like this at your wedding," Stacey suggested.

Kenny glanced at me and I knew he was thinking of the menu plans I'd worked so hard to get exactly right and was struggling to think of the right thing to say. I had to help him out.

"It would be brilliant if we could, Stacey, but I don't think we can. You see, we are the only people in the whole world who know the special recipe we invented to make these cakes. I'm going to be too busy getting married to make them and I was rather hoping you'd be busy too."

"Busy doing what?"

"Being my bridesmaid."

"Really? Wow! I'd love to. I can wear a dress like a princess and my necklace and tiara and your shiny sandals."

"Lovely," I managed to say.

I wonder if my mum or Aunty Betty have any tips for tactfully getting a seven-year-old to rethink her choice of accessories.

4. One-Upmanship

My cousin Becky has always considered herself a cut above me. Gives herself airs and graces, she does. Reckon she gets that from her mum. The whole lot of them are pretty stuck up, actually. Take summat simple, like introducing us girls to anyone. If me mum wanted you to meet me, she'd just say, "This is me daughter, Angie Smith. Ange, stop chewing an' say 'ello will yer?"

Becky's mum always did it different. "May I introduce you to my daughter? Rebecca Harrington-Smith. Rebecca, darling, do say hello."

Then Becky would pipe up. "Pleased to meet you," she'd come out with. If it was a bloke she was talking to, she'd even go and throw in a 'sir'.

Come to think of it, they're just the same now. If she'd had her way, no one would even know we're related. Her mum wouldn't of owned up, I mean. Becky's not much different though.

"Angela, please don't call me Becky. I prefer to be called Rebecca," she kept saying at school.

What the stuck up cow meant was, "Don't speak to me, Angie; you're far too common."

Used to ask if I wanted to do me homework with her. I didn't. I had far more interesting stuff to do. There was a shopping centre to hang about in and boys to snog; I didn't have time for boring schoolwork.

That was when we were kids, like. Things is different now. Both of us got kids of our own now; two apiece. That's about all we've got in common though. She, Becky I mean, married some snooty chap with shed loads of cash. Well, she would've wouldn't she? Brags about him all the flippin' time, she does. Invites me round to that swanky house of hers, too.

"Please do come for tea, Angela. I'd love to see you."

What she means is, she'd love to show off how much better than me she's doing.

"We're family, we should help each other out," she says as she gives me her cast offs. She's just hoping to keep me sweet, so I don't go embarrassing her in public.

"Please bring the boys round for a dip in the pool," she used to say every summer. Just her way of hinting she didn't think our lot washed properly, I reckon. Always wanting to compare the kids too, she was.

"Sebastian is really enjoying his music lessons; perhaps your Trevor would like to join him?"

Well, no he wouldn't. My Trevor liked to play his ghetto blaster as loud as it'd go, he didn't need no fancy clarinet or whatever it was called.

"I've hired a private tutor to help the children with their schoolwork, maybe your boys would like to join them for some lessons?"

I expect you can guess the answer to that. That's right; they had better things to do with their time.

She didn't give up the family traditions of snobbery neither. Only became a bleedin' magistrate didn't she? How soft can you get? Always going on about law and order and rules and regulations, that lot. Obsessed like. Even mention stuff that everyone's into; pirate videos, duty free fags, adding a bit to an insurance claim, that kind of thing, she starts on as if I'm some kind of flippin' criminal.

Bit of a social climber too, if you know what I mean. Anyone with a title, or swanky job, she'll hang around 'em like they was summat special. I wouldn't of done that, even if I'd got the chance.

When she wasn't going on about her posh friends, she'd bore me to tears about her darling kids. Her Sebastian turned out to be pretty good on that poncey instrument of his. Even got to play for Princess Michael of Kent once, he did. As you'd imagine, Becky went on and on about it. Sent us pictures, all sorts. The other boy became some fancy scientist, with one of them long names hardly anyone can say. Does some tests for the police, apparently.

Anyway, it's about time I got to the point of this little story. I've finally got one over on Becky. I thought of ringing her up and telling her straight away. Thought better of it though; I want to see her face when I break the news. You're wondering what's happened aren't you? Oh, go on then, I'll tell yer. I suppose I can trust you not to spill the beans.

I'm meeting her for coffee. The plan is to get her talking about them precious kids of hers and then I'll break it to her.

"You think your kids are real impressive don't you? One of 'em does a few odd jobs for the local coppers and the other played a couple of tunes for some two-bit royal hanger on," that's what I'll say and she'll get that look on her face. You know the one I mean, like she's better 'an everyone else an' her farts smell of strawberries. She'll lean forward, as if to tell me to get on with it. Then I'll tell her.

"Well, my two lads are right now helping CID with some very important enquiries, and the copper what told me, said as they were likely to be spending at least ten years at her Majesty's pleasure!"

5. First Step

Jacqueline stepped out of the taxi and looked up at the impressive façade of Winterdean House. She sighed.

"You all right, love?" the driver asked.

"Yes, fine thanks. It's just that we're moving soon and I'll miss this place."

"Going somewhere nice?" he asked as he retrieved her shopping from the boot.

"That new tower block they've just finished, on Queen Street."

The driver glanced at the beautiful sprawling mansion. "Crikey, that'll be a bit of a difference!"

She nodded. He was right; it would be very different from the life she was used to.

"I hope you'll be happy there."

"I'm sure we will, thanks."

"Watch how you go now."

As she walked across the gravel forecourt, Jacqueline couldn't avoid making comparisons between her current home and the flat she would soon be living in. There'd be no ringing for taxis or muddy driveways to negotiate for a start. The tower block was right in town, so many of the places she'd want to visit would be within walking distance. When that wasn't the case, she could get the bus. The flats, unlike Winterdean House, were situated on a bus route. Jacqueline supposed the convenience would compensate for the lost luxury of a taxi to herself.

Winterdean House had been her home for almost four years. She and James had never lived together anywhere else. Their daughter had never lived anywhere else at all. It seemed very likely the child's first steps would be taken in the new place. Although Jacqueline had spent all her free time lately sorting through their possessions and packing for the move, it was still difficult to believe that in just two days they would be living in a modern flat. Well, two bedrooms and a tiny space for a cot. She patted her belly; the new baby would be born just a month after they moved in.

The park close to their new home would take the place of the lawns and flower beds Jacqueline had become used to. She and James had walked round the park before their appointment to view the flat. It was beautiful and she'd learnt that although the grass was cut by the council, the flower beds were tended by local volunteers. It was a delightful place and bigger than the gardens she was used to. Better kept too since Hugh, the gardener, had left Winterdean House. He'd got a live-in job in Wales, good pay and a private apartment for him and his family. Jacqueline had wished him well; she didn't begrudge him going to a better position.

Jacqueline was glad that Lucy, the nursery nurse, was also moving to the new place. Jacqueline's daughter loved Lucy and was happy left in her care. Jacqueline knew she could trust her with the new baby too.

Not everyone was leaving. Maggie, the cleaner, would be staying. She'd been at Winterdean for years, since before James had arrived even. Luke the chef was staying behind, too. He'd probably make his wonderful treacle tart for whoever moved in to take her place. It was hard to think of someone else welcoming friends through her front door, or looking out of her favourite window, but of course there soon would be. Maggie and Luke and the others would make the new people welcome, just as they'd made her welcome when she'd moved into James's old home. Jacqueline went straight to the kitchen to drop off her bags.

"Kettle's on. Fancy a cuppa?" Luke asked.

"Oooh, yes please, I need one, but I'd better go and reclaim my daughter first; Lucy will want some peace to finish her own packing."

"Right-o," Luke said. "Can you manage a slice of treacle tart?" He didn't wait for an answer before cutting a generous wedge.

"I'm going to miss you, Luke."

"You'll be fine. That new kitchen of yours will be easy to keep clean and you'll be able to cook what you want, when you want, without me or anyone else getting in your way."

"True. There'll only be room for one person at a time in there."

He was right though; the whole flat would be easy to clean. She'd easily manage on her own. The compact cooker and neat microwave would be easier to use than the huge range from Winterdean House too. James had carefully explained their financial situation to her and they'd gone through all the various options. Moving really was the best thing to do, Jacqueline reassured herself as she climbed the stairs in search of Lucy. She and James would miss Luke and Maggie and the others, but they'd have new neighbours. They'd soon settle in and make friends.

"She almost took a step, just now," Lucy told her. "She stood all on her own and lifted her foot. Stayed like that for what seemed ages before crashing down on her bottom."

"She'll do it any day now. Probably be running round

whilst I'm trying to unpack. Talking of packing, how are you getting on?"

Lucy assured her that hers was almost done. "What about you?"

"I'm almost ready, just a few toys and our washing things to be added," Jacqueline said.

"Look, she's doing it again," Lucy interrupted.

Jacqueline watched as her daughter stood confidently on one leg, moved the raised one slightly forward and promptly sat down again.

"I hope our first steps on the property ladder go better than that," Jacqueline said, before returning to the kitchen for her tea and treacle tart. It would be strange moving out of the bedsit at Winterdean House, but she was looking forward to moving into the flat she and James were buying.

6. Mum Knows Best

Jeremy was very good at giving advice. Whenever his mates were faced with any kind of dilemma they'd come to see him. He was always pleased to help out, as Mum always said, 'a friend in need is a friend indeed'.

"You've got to help me," one of his friends in need had called after him one day.

Jeremy had been walking round to his dear Fran's flat to take her a bunch of flowers, but he stopped to listen to the problem.

"I've got two cute girls on the go and the guilt and secrecy are driving me mad and… "

"Come on mate," Jeremy interrupted. "That's not on. You'll have to work out which one you care most about and then let the other one know it's over. You can't go around lying and cheating; it simply isn't fair."

"But Jez, they're both lovely… "

"If they're lovely, they deserve the truth."

"But I can't choose."

"You can't really be in love with two women."

"I am, I am."

"So much in love you lie?"

"All right, all right. I'll do the right thing."

His friend had chosen one girl and let the other down as gently as possible. Jeremy was pleased; as his mum always said, 'honesty is the best policy'.

It wasn't just his friends that he helped. When his cousin

rang up distressed, Jeremy went straight round to see him.

"I think I'm going to lose my girlfriend. She says I've got fat and lazy."

"Well, you have," Jeremy pointed out. "You smoke, eat and drink far too much. You need to cut down."

"But I love my fags, beer and burgers."

"Love them more than a healthy body and healthy relationship?"

"Well, no. I suppose not."

"You have to decide which is more important. In my opinion, there's no contest. As my mum always says, 'if you've not got your health you don't have anything.' You're going to give up smoking and start a diet. Some exercise would be a good idea too."

"But, Jerry, I don't know if I can."

"You can. Don't worry, I'll help you."

Jeremy did help. He helped a lot, because as his mum always said, 'blood is thicker than water'.

It was whilst he was accompanying his cousin to aerobics classes that Jeremy met Claudia. She was just lovely. To his delight, she seemed to feel exactly the same way about him.

One evening after a date with Claudia, Jeremy came home to find another of his friends sat on his doorstep with an overnight bag by his side.

"Jezzer, can I stay with you for a bit?"

"Of course you can. Come in and tell me what's up."

Over coffee, his friend explained that his fiancée and his mother didn't get on.

"I ended up having a blazing row with both of them. I told the girlfriend not to upset my mother so she kicked me out. I went round to Mother's and told her she was to blame and she sent me away with a flea in my ear."

That night, Jeremy remembered another of his mum's sayings; 'there's two sides to every argument'. He visited his friend's fiancée and mother.

"Hasn't got time for his old mum now he's got that girl," his friend's mother said.

"He's supposed to be living with me, but he's always going round to his mum's for meals or taking her shopping," was the fiancée's opinion.

Before going round to visit dear Fran, Jeremy told his friend, "You need to get them together. It's no good constantly splitting yourself between the two and keeping them apart. Take your fiancée with you when you go round your mum's or invite her to your place."

"But mate, they won't get along."

"At least give them the chance to get to know each other."

"They've got absolutely nothing in common."

"They've got you."

Two weeks later, Jeremy was getting ready for a date with Claudia when the friend who'd been staying with him rang up. "Fancy going to the football on Saturday, Jezzer?"

"Oh dear, don't tell me you're on your own again?" Jeremy asked. He was sure that things would have worked out OK between his friend's fiancée and mother as they both seemed such nice people.

"Yes, mate. My mother and the girlfriend are going shopping; looking at wedding dresses would you believe?"

Jeremy did believe it, because as his mum always said, 'love conquers all'.

Jeremy wasn't very good at taking advice, not even his

own. He lied to both Fran and Claudia and felt guilty about it. Although he tried to split himself between the two of them, it didn't really work; they were beginning to get suspicious. In trying to keep up the pretence, his health and diet were suffering. Often he'd be invited to a superb roast beef dinner complete with Yorkshire puddings, roast potatoes and rich gravy, followed by plum crumble at Fran's flat on Sunday lunch-time, then he'd arrive at Claudia's and be presented with onion bhaji, followed with dahl biriyani and all the trimmings, washed down with ice cold lager the same evening.

He decided he couldn't keep up the deception any longer; it wasn't fair either to him or to them. Knowing that honesty is the best policy didn't help him choose between the two. He had to do that himself.

He called Fran. "We need to talk, my dear."

"Great idea, why don't you come to lunch?"

When he arrived, she hugged and kissed him before pouring glasses of full-bodied red wine. "You make yourself comfortable and I'll just put your steak under the grill. I won't be a moment."

He sat on her cream leather sofa and looked around him. Everywhere there were reminders of things they'd done together. On the mantelpiece was a photograph of the two of them on a sunny beach. Her CD collection included albums she'd bought after concerts they'd gone to together. The crystal flower vase in the window was a birthday gift from him.

Fran sat on the sofa beside him. "That'll take care of itself for a while. It's great to have you to myself for a change. So, tell me, what did you want to talk about?"

How could he hurt his dearest Fran?

"Not much. It was just an excuse to spend more time with you."

When it began to get dark, Jeremy left. He had to; he'd told Claudia he'd be round after playing golf with his mates. He ran all the way there, tripping and landing on his shoulder in his haste. He was rubbing it as she opened the door.

"Oh dear, you poor thing. Have you been overdoing it?"

Claudia played soothing music and began to unbutton his shirt. Soon she was massaging his sore shoulder with fragrant oils.

"It's a good thing you've got me to look after you," she whispered as her fingers worked their magic.

He couldn't give her up, he just couldn't.

Jeremy was still undecided and unhappy when his mum phoned him a week later.

"About my birthday barbecue, darling, could you tell me if there's anything special that Claudia will want to eat?"

"About that, I'm not sure if I'll be able to make it after all."

"Not come to your mum's fiftieth birthday party? Of course, you'll find a way, darling. Blood is thicker than water after all."

"Yes, Mum, I'll be there, but I'm not sure Claudia will be able to come," said Jeremy who hadn't invited her.

"Yes she will, darling. I bumped into her in town earlier and she's looking forward to it."

"Oh."

"Would you be able to pick up Fran on your way over? She's bringing most of the food. The dear girl is supplying it from her shop. I don't want her carrying it and hurting her back though. You know what I always say, if you haven't got your health you haven't got anything."

"That's right, Mum, you do. Er, did you mention Fran when you spoke to Claudia."

"No, dear. I didn't. That's up to you. I really can't believe you haven't told them the truth. Honesty really is the best policy you know."

So, Jeremy told Fran and Claudia the truth. They both came to the party. Jeremy was relieved at how well Claudia, his vegetarian girlfriend, got along with his sister Fran, even though Fran made no secret of her job as a butcher. He really shouldn't have been surprised; hadn't Mum always told him that love conquers all?

7. Reunion

"The weather forecast is good for next weekend," Sean said as he cleared the table after Sunday breakfast. "Fancy a few days away in the caravan?

"Mmm, we could take the kids to Curracloe," Clare said.

"It's a great beach for kids," Sean agreed. "But it's a long way… "

"Oh, Daddy, please can we go to Currychloe seaside?"

"Please, please, please."

Laughing, Sean gave in to his daughters' pleading. "OK, but I can't help feeling I've been ambushed."

"We're going to bury you in the sand!" the girls promised. They ran out to their sandpit to practise.

"So why Curracloe?" Sean asked. "Trying to relive your youth?"

"Like you said, it's a great beach for kids."

Clare took the dishes into the kitchen. She hadn't lied; it really was a great beach. Clare and her elder sister had spent half of every school holiday there. Their grandparents lived next to the grandparents of two boys. They'd become friends when the girls challenged the boys to build a better sandcastle than them. The first summer the four of them spent the whole holiday together. The boys had taught the girls to skim stones and fly kites. The girls had told the boys about the knights and princesses who lived in the castles of sand.

In later years their older siblings lost interest in such

31

childish entertainments and preferred to read or sunbathe. Jim and Clare had built castles and a lasting friendship.

When they were fifteen they knew their shared holidays were over and they'd both wondered about the future. They'd skimmed stones to 'see' the future.

"Odds is no, evens is yes," Jim declared. "Will I pass my exams?"

He threw a pebble and they watched it skip over the surface of the water four times. "Yes! Now you try, Clare."

Her stone bounced twice.

They'd learned he'd be abducted by aliens but wouldn't go bald. Her teeth would fall out and she'd own a sports car.

"I'll take you for a drive," she promised. "That's if the aliens bring you back."

"All right." They shook on it.

"Pity we don't really know what will happen," Jim said.

"We do about some things."

"Like what?"

"That we'll always be friends."

"I hope so, but people lose touch." He threw a stone. It bounced four times. "I know, let's promise to meet right here in exactly twenty years," Jim said

"Like in a film? OK and if neither of us is married, we'll marry each other exactly a year after that."

"What if we are married?"

"Then our children will be best friends, just like we are."

It had been a pact. They'd sealed it by sharing a last ice cream and first kiss.

They'd met again twelve years ago at his grandmother's funeral. She'd hardly got a chance to talk to Jim. Good came of the sad occasion though; she'd spoken to Sean and learnt he lived close to her. He'd given her a lift home and their romance began.

She hadn't seen Jim for far too long as he now lived on the east coast – of Scotland. He'd attended her wedding, of course.

Clare told Sean about the pact as they left for their honeymoon.

He'd laughed. "You've been secretly engaged to Jim all this time?"

"Yes. Well, not engaged but we did have an agreement. I know it sounds silly now, but it seemed… "

"Like a good idea at the time," Sean finished for her.

That was years ago. He'd probably forgotten about it by now. Maybe she could slip off on her own and meet up with Jim?

On Friday, Clare fussed over her packing. She couldn't decide what to wear to meet Jim. A swimsuit and shorts? He'd been used to seeing her like that. Conscious she was no longer the skinny, blonde-haired, sun-kissed girl she once was, she packed an alternative outfit. That was silly, for all Clare knew he'd forgotten their pact and she'd be left standing on the beach, waiting alone for a man who wasn't coming. No; she knew he'd be there.

On Saturday, the day she'd arranged to meet Jim, Clare said, "Go on, you three, go fly your kites whilst I clear up from breakfast and have a quick shower."

She dressed in a casual summer dress. It was a natural choice for the beach, hid her stretch marks, and the colour suited her too. Not that it mattered, but actually she looked pretty good. She wondered if Jim had changed. Would he still be as slim and would his hair be as thick and dark as she remembered?

Clare set off to find the man she'd loved for years and tell him the truth.

"Sean, you remember that pact I made with Jim?"

"Something daft, about if neither of you married, you'd get together?" he answered, still watching the girls and trying to untangle the string from his own kite.

"Yes. Today is the day we agreed to meet on Curracloe beach."

He dropped the knotted string. "I really have been ambushed! You're not actually going through with it?"

"Of course, I made a promise."

"And you always keep your promises." It wasn't quite a question.

"Yes, I keep promises, stick to pacts and remember my wedding vows."

He put his arms around her. "Of course you do, love. It's just that I know how close you and Jim were and …"

She kissed him. "So, it's OK?"

"If that's what you want, then yes. It will seem weird though."

"It'll be fun, you'll see. Anyway it will be nice for us all to have a family day out at the seaside."

"All of us?"

"Yes, that was the deal; if we had families we'd introduce them. You will come?"

"Wouldn't miss it for anything."

Leaving Sean to follow with kites and children, Clare walked towards the beach. She saw Jim was already at the water's edge, skimming stones. Did he still ask questions before releasing them, just as she did? The only way to know was to ask. She scrambled down the same footpath they'd always used to meet him. At least she didn't have to worry about recognising him.

They hugged.

He picked her up and swung her round. "Have you brought your family with you?"

"Yes, you?"

"Yes, I said I'd wave when we want them."

Clare laughed. "Me too."

They both waved at their respective families.

"You haven't changed a bit since I last saw you," she said.

"Neither have you."

"Aww, get away with you. Never notice anything you; you're as bad as your brother."

"Actually, I think you'll find he's far worse than me," Sean said. "It's great to see you, Jim; we've all missed you. But enough of that, there are more important things to worry about. I bet my kids can build a much better sandcastle than your lot can."

"That's hardly fair; you know we have pebbles not sand up our way," Jim protested.

"Then yours will have an advantage in skimming stones," Clare said. It wouldn't be a big one though, she'd taught her girls well.

8. The Toddler Diet

Jemima looked down at the dial on the bathroom scales and blinked. She stepped off, moved them away from the wall and tried again. She knelt and fiddled with the little wheel at the back to ensure the red mark was exactly over the zero then confirmed the first reading. There was no doubt about it; time to buy some new clothes.

Two weeks ago, she remembered, she'd been complaining to her elder sister about her weight problem.

"It's just not fair, Morgan. I've tried everything to lose weight."

"Everything?"

"Yes, everything."

"Ever fing," Jeremy, Morgan's son, added.

"OK, maybe not everything, but lots of things. I tried not eating after seven in the evening, then food combining, then eating seven tiny meals a day. Those plans were followed by the low GI diet. I had a go at that thing where you have grapefruit with every meal and the one where you eat savoury food one day and sweet the next. None of them helped."

Jeremy went back to his colouring book.

"I know it's a complete last resort, but have you thought of just eating less and exercising more?" Morgan asked.

"I have tried, but it's impossible for me. You can't talk, lying back on the sofa with your cream cheese and chocolate fingers. No one makes comments about any weight you gain."

"I'm only eating this because of my cravings," Morgan said as she scooped up the last of the garlic and herb cheese with a milk chocolate biscuit. "Anyway, I'll make sure I lose the weight after the birth."

"Yeah, right."

"I have done that before. Twice."

"Of course you have, Sis. Sorry, it's just that it doesn't seem fair. We used to eat the same and look about the same when we both lived at home. Now you eat loads and look great, even with your bump. I look chubby, even though I'm on a permanent diet."

"You look fine."

"Stand up, here next to me."

Morgan did as instructed.

Jemima pointed out their reflection in the window. "We look like bookends!"

"You're sticking your belly out."

"I'm fat."

"And I've got swollen ankles. Honestly, Sis, if you're so bothered about it, join a gym or something and lose the weight." Morgan returned to the sofa and stretched out. "Or if you think it's all easy for me, then you have kids too."

"What! No way; talk about last resort; that's a crazy idea."

"It's not. You said it yourself, we both used to be chubby and now I'm not. You remember Mum telling to us not to worry about a bit of puppy fat, because she'd been the same and lost it once she had kids?"

"Yeah, vaguely, but that was just to cheer us up."

"I think it's true. A genetic thing, maybe. Once women in

our family have a kid, they lose weight."

Jemima shook her head and started to do star jumps. "You've convinced me… exercise… it is," she panted out as she leapt repeatedly into the air.

Morgan chuckled. Jeremy rushed over and tried to imitate Jemima's movements. He laughed as his chubby fist collided with his aunt's arm. Morgan stifled giggles by putting her hands over her mouth. Jemima laughed too, but continued with the exercises. Morgan bent over and wrapped her arms under her legs, whilst her body shook.

Jemima stopped jumping. "Don't overreact, Sis. I don't look that funny."

Morgan looked up, her face white. "It's the baby… "

"Not baby," Jeremy protested.

"The new baby, love," Morgan explained.

"It can't be! It's not due for months and Peter's away." Jemima put her arm round her sister.

Morgan sat up. "I'm OK now, but for a minute, I really did think I was going into labour. Perhaps it was just heartburn from all that cheese?"

"You're OK now, though?"

"'Kay, Mummy?"

"Yes, love. I'm fine really. Sorry if I scared you."

"You did a bit," her sister admitted.

"Film?" Jeremy asked.

"Not now love, but you can watch the *Telletubbies* for a little while.

"I'll do it," Jemima said. She put the video into the machine and set the volume on low. She looked into her niece's carry cot. "Sleeps through everything, doesn't she?"

"Everything except dawn. She's an angel as long as you like getting up really early. Come on then, tell me what exercises you're going to try. Do me a favour though; don't make me laugh."

"I thought of getting some exercise DVDs, then I could do them at home without looking like an idiot."

"Good idea, anyone who sees the martyred look on your face is liable to do themselves a mischief laughing at you."

"Thanks a lot!" Jemima threw a cushion towards her sister.

"Ow!"

"It didn't touch you. Hey Morgan, have you got that pain again?"

Morgan nodded and bent over. "It really does feel like a contraction. I think I should go to hospital, just in case."

"Do you want me to drive you in?"

"No, I want you to call a taxi, help me pack a few things and then stay here with the kids."

"Uh oh. OK. Should I call Peter?"

"Not until I know for sure. It'll be really difficult for him to come back early."

By the time they'd packed a bag and Morgan had explained to Jeremy that she was going to see a doctor and Aunty Jemima was going to look after him and his sister, the taxi had arrived.

"He got here quick," Morgan said. Another pain gripped her as she stepped outside.

"Take her straight from here to maternity," Jemima said.

Once the taxi was out of sight, Jemima turned her attention to occupying Jeremy. "Would you like to watch your film now?" she asked.

"No. More jumping!"

The exercise and following exhaustion certainly helped take her mind of her worries about Morgan. Fortunately, Jeremy got puffed out before Jemima collapsed completely and was then content to go back to his colouring while she fixed them a plate of sandwiches.

Morgan called from the hospital to say the staff had managed to stop her contractions and the baby seemed fine. "I have to stay in for a while though and Peter won't be back for two weeks."

"Don't worry; I'll look after the kids. I've already phoned work and said I might not be in tomorrow. They said I can take my leave now if I want to."

"Are you sure you'll be OK?"

"Yeah, I've babysat loads of times."

"Looking after them full-time is different."

"I'll be fine."

"Where Mummy?" a trembling voice asked as Jemima replaced the receiver.

"She's gone to have some things done for the new baby. I'm looking after you and Susi for a little while, won't that be fun?"

"Yeah! Film?"

"OK, Jeremy. I suppose you want, *Finding Nemo*?"

Jemima gave Susi a bottle, while they watched the film.

"Tea time," Jeremy declared as soon as it finished.

"But we've just had a plate of sandwiches." Or rather he had, Jemima hadn't fancied chocolate spread on bread which smelt of garlic.

"Ungry. Tea time."

"OK, what would you like to eat?"

"Oops."

"What's that?"

"Oops." Jeremy sounded annoyed.

Jemima went into the kitchen and looked in the cupboards. She found several small tins of spaghetti hoops.

"Jeremy, is this it? Spaghetti hoops?"

"Oops," he agreed.

Jemima warmed some up and was rewarded with a beaming smile when she placed the dish in front of him.

"Oops, oops."

He ate nearly as many as he got in his hair, on the floor, over his clothes and on Jemima.

"I think I'm going to have to bath you, young man."

Before she could, Susi began to cry. Jemima changed her and gave her another bottle. She put the girl into her cot and bathed Jeremy. After reading him a story, she put him to bed too.

Jemima opened the fridge door in search of food for herself. Everything smelt of the garlic cheese her sister was currently so fond of. The cupboards were full of different types of baby food, spaghetti hoops and little else. Jemima ate a chocolate finger and imagined it tasted of garlic. She gave up on food and cleaned the spaghetti covered floor and put Jeremy's clothes on to wash. Then she had an early night; she'd remembered Morgan's warning about dawn starts.

At five-thirty, Jemima was giving Susi another bottle and asking Jeremy what he would like for breakfast.

"Oops."

"Not for breakfast, surely?"

"Oops." He was using the annoyed voice again.

"You can have them for lunch. How about some Rice Crispies for breakfast?"

"OOPS!"

"OK, hoops it is."

While Jeremy ate his spaghetti, Jemima poured garlic flavoured milk over Rice Crispies. She didn't eat them all.

During the course of the day Jemima heated up spaghetti hoops twice more, cleaned the kitchen floor three times, watched *Finding Nemo* again, went to the park twice, fed Susi copious amounts of pureed gunk and milk and changed lots of nappies. She tasted most of the contents of the fridge before throwing them and the garlic cheese in the bin. After bathing Jeremy, she had an early night.

"We're going to have to go shopping, today," Jemima said the following morning as she opened the last tin of spaghetti hoops.

"Weets?"

"If you mean sweets, then OK, if you're really good. What else would you like to do today?"

"Wings."

"OK, we'll go to the park and I'll push you on the swings before we go shopping."

"Mummy?"

"You want to see Mummy?"

Jemima took her niece and nephew to the park then phoned her sister.

"Good grief, I didn't expect to ever hear from you before

nine in the morning," Morgan said, laughing.

"Nine is now the time I go to bed, not when I get up."

"Yeah, kids are like that. How are you coping?"

"OK. I never want to see spaghetti hoops again and I've already resorted to bribing Jeremy with sweets if he's good when we go shopping."

"A few won't hurt him if you brush his teeth afterwards. Shopping with kids is harder than doing it on your own."

"I guessed it would be. Can we visit you afterwards?"

"That would be great."

"Mima, Mima."

Jemima opened her eyes. She was sprawled on the sofa with Jeremy tugging her hand.

"Tea time. Oops," he said.

Jemima could barely remember the shopping trip, hospital visit and second trip to the park. The open box on the floor suggested that she'd put *Finding Nemo* on before falling asleep.

She heated two tins of spaghetti; she'd been so concerned with remembering everything she needed for Susi and preventing Jeremy selecting too many sweets that she'd forgotten to buy herself any food.

After ten days, getting up at five-thirty in the morning seemed almost normal and half a tin of spaghetti hoops was considered a proper meal. On the fourteenth day, when Peter rang to say he was at the airport and she could return to her normal life in a couple of hours, she wasn't quite sure what her life used to be like.

After hugging her and thanking her for caring for the

children, Peter took a proper look at Jemima.

"Your latest diet is sure working wonders."

"Thanks, Peter. I'm going home to bed. See you later."

Waking up, Jemima remembered Peter's words. What diet? There hadn't been time to think about dieting; Peter was probably just being nice. It wouldn't hurt to step on the scales though.

Jemima looked down at the dial on the bathroom scales and blinked. She stepped off, moved them away from the wall and tried again. She bent down and fiddled with the little wheel at the back to ensure the red mark was exactly over the zero and confirmed the first reading. There was no doubt about it; she'd lost half a stone!

Jemima rang Peter. "I'll come back this afternoon and watch the kids while you visit Morgan if you like and in the evenings, so you can go shopping and at the weekends too."

"It would be a great help if you can, but I've got to say, you're a real glutton for punishment."

"No I'm not. I've just discovered Mum was right; having kids really is a great way to lose weight."

9. Don't Say Goodbye

Meera's concentration on the local news programme was broken by the sound of angry voices. She continued to watch the charity cyclist wave and call goodbye to his supporters but didn't catch where he was going or when he'd be back.

"It's not fair!" Sonia, her granddaughter, shouted.

"Life isn't fair," the deeper voice of Sonia's father yelled back.

This was followed by the sound of someone stamping down the stairs and leaving the house, slamming the front door behind them.

Slower, quieter footsteps followed. Meera glanced up from her seat on the sofa. Her son looked tired.

"I don't know how to talk to that girl anymore. We argued about a boy she's been seen with and now she's stormed off into the rain with no coat and she didn't even say goodbye."

"I suppose she'll have taken that mobile of hers with her?"

"Yes, but she probably won't answer if I call her."

Meera shook her head. This family argument reminded her of a much earlier one. That time it had been Meera and her own father who'd shouted about a boyfriend of Meera's. Since her husband's death three years previously, she'd often thought of the man to whom she'd never said goodbye. With modern mobile phones, emails and the internet it should be so easy for people to communicate, but it seemed just as difficult as it had always been.

"Send her one of those text things and ask her to come and

talk to me."

A few minutes later, Sonia returned.

Meera held out a hand to her granddaughter. "What's not fair?"

"Oh, Nana. Dad has banned me from seeing Adam!"

"Oh, my poor child, come here." Was history repeating itself?

Sonia sank to the ground and rested her head on Meera's lap.

"Who is this Adam?" Meera asked.

"You remember the plumber who put in the shower?"

"Yes. A nice man, but too old for you, my dear."

"No, Nana. It's his son. His real name is Dobroslav Adamczyk, but everyone calls him either Adam if they're his friend or XYZ, if they're not."

"XYZ?"

"It's supposed to be a joke, just because his name's Polish and looks difficult to say."

"And your father has banned you from seeing this Polish boy?"

"I'm not allowed to phone him, or email him or anything."

Meera stroked the girl's dark hair. "I thought I'd raised him better than that. When the same thing happened to me, I vowed that no one in my family would... I'll have a word with him and see if I can get him to be more reasonable."

"Thank you, Nana."

"While I do that, don't you think you should be getting on with your homework?"

"Oh, Nana!" Sonia slouched off to her room.

Meera went in search of her son. "Sonia tells me you've banned her from seeing that boy Adam."

"Why can't she ever listen to me?"

"Because you're being totally unreasonable?"

"I just want what's best for her."

"You want what you think is best," Meera said.

"You don't think she should be making the most of her education, then?"

"Of course I do, but that's not what this is about. You can't choose your daughter's friends for her. If you try, you'll just drive her away, the same as happened to me and my father."

"Mother, this isn't anything like the same. I told Sonia that I don't want her going out in the evenings when she has school the following day and that she's not to log onto the internet chat rooms until she's finished her homework."

"And what about Adam?"

"Sonia seems infatuated with him, but she's young. I imagine that will wear off eventually."

"And if it doesn't?"

He shrugged. "He's a nice enough lad and in any case, it's her decision."

"I'll talk to her again."

Meera tapped on her granddaughter's bedroom door. "Sonia, love, I want to tell you about a boy I knew when I was about your age," Meera said.

"Are you going to try to get me to give up Adam?"

"No, quite the opposite. The boy I knew was called Tony. I had a Saturday job in a shop, that's how I met him. He took me to the pictures once and my father found out. He banned me from seeing him."

"Nana, that's awful! He broke your heart."

"No. We were just friends really and I don't suppose we'd have been anything else, but I was so angry with my father, that I didn't explain. Instead I acted as though he'd ruined my life. When I argued, he made me leave my job too, so I couldn't see Tony there. I never got to say goodbye. I never really forgave my father for that, even though I knew he was doing what he thought was best for me."

"Like Dad does with me; that's what you mean, isn't it?"

"Yes, but your father isn't like mine. He hasn't banned you from seeing this boy, just asked you to put your education first. Maybe your relationship with Adam will last and maybe it won't but if it doesn't, you won't be denied the chance to say goodbye."

"No. I suppose I'd better go and apologise to Dad for overreacting. Did you never hear from Tony again or find out what happened to him?"

"No, well I don't think so. When I heard you and your dad arguing, I'd just seen the local news. There was a man with the same name who was beginning a charity cycle ride. The Tony I knew was a keen cyclist... "

"It could be the same man."

"It could, but I'm not likely to bump into him now if it hasn't happened in the last fifty years and he probably won't remember me anyway."

Meera watched the news the next evening, but there was no further coverage of the charity cycle ride. She asked Sonia to look up on the internet about the charity he'd raised money for. There was an article on the website that described his trip, but gave no further details about him.

"Never mind, I was just curious."

Despite her words, Meera thought Tony might remember her. It was true they had never been anything other than friends, but they had been good friends. They'd talked and talked about everything and they'd laughed. They'd laughed together more in those few months than Meera had in the years since then.

"Did you talk to your father?" she asked Sonia.

"Yes, Nana. We had a long chat and he's agreed I can see Adam on the weekends and one evening per week, as long as I say where we're going, I'm not out late and keep up with my school work."

Meera left Sonia to continue using the computer for her own purposes and went back to her favourite spot on the living room sofa.

"Nana, come and have a look at this," Sonia called an hour later.

"What is it?"

"An email for you."

"For me? Who would email me?"

"His name is Tony. I contacted the charity and asked them to pass on a message asking if he remembered you. He's just replied to say he does and would like to hear from you. He says he always wondered what happened."

"What should I say?" Meera asked.

"You told me you wanted the chance to say goodbye, but I think it might be better to start with hello and take it from there."

10. Growing Up

Robyn imagined she could hear the train rumbling towards her. She couldn't. It wasn't due for another twenty minutes.

The sinking sun did little to warm her as she waited on the wooden bench on the draughty station. She remembered other summer afternoons.; when the only decisions she had to worry about were which flavour crisps she wanted with her picnic tea. The whole family had been together then; Mum, Dad and Robyn. She'd been a happy child. At fifteen, Robyn should still have been a child, but she wasn't.

Eight months ago baby Helen had arrived and things had begun to go wrong. Robyn loved the child but she didn't want to spend every minute she wasn't at school caring for the infant. She wanted to go out, see friends, have fun.

There'd been so many rows at home; most of them between Robyn and her mother. Dad stayed quiet. Far too quiet.

Mother and daughter argued about staying out late, drinking, smoking.

"Where the hell have you been?"

"None of your business."

"You could at least have had the decency to let one of us know you'd be late so we weren't lying awake worrying half the night."

"Worry? You? All you're worried about is what the neighbours will think."

"No, I'm worried about you. You can hardly stand,

anything could have happened to you."

"Well nothing did. Like you said, I can't stand, so I'm going to bed."

Often she'd not made it to bed and had slept on the sofa.

They'd argued about sharing responsibility for household tasks and caring for little Helen.

"I'm not the only one with a working pair of hands in this house."

"Cook a meal once in a while can't you, instead of lecturing me about how difficult it is to combine school work and looking after a kid."

They'd screamed and shouted, hurt and been hurt. The rows had stopped abruptly; you can't argue with someone who's never there, who won't speak to you.

Dad had never argued. Perhaps he should have. Instead he pleaded.

"Please try to understand, love," he'd said. "She's young, it's difficult. Can't we just go back to how things used to be?"

They couldn't of course.

Running away wasn't an answer, she knew that, but it had stopped the rows, removed some of the pressures of family life for a time.

Robyn checked her watch; five minutes to go. In five minutes time she really would hear the train's approach. She had until then to decide whether to stay or go, to work out if she could live with her mother or not. Fifteen was too young to make such a decision, far too young. Fifteen was too young to care for a child, too young to lose family support, too young to cope with drinking and late nights.

Dad had asked her to understand. She hadn't, she hadn't

even tried; until now. Robyn thought about how things used to be. However much her dad wanted it, they couldn't change what had happened and go back to that – could they? Of course they couldn't. Things changed, people changed, perhaps even Robyn and her mum? Robyn knew she had. Since she'd not had her mum to shop and clean, she realised how much work had been done for her. She saw how hard it was to face up to responsibility and that running away from one problem just caused another. Most importantly she saw there was blame on both sides and that she could apologise – and forgive.

The sound of rapidly approaching feet made Robyn look behind her. It was just a stranger, hurrying onto the platform, fumbling with change for the ticket machine. He reminded her of her dad. Poor Dad, he'd wanted to come in the car and take all his family back home.

"It would be too much pressure with you and Helen there too. I need to know I'm making my own decision. You can wait in the station car park, so you'll be right there when the train comes."

She didn't know if he understood, but he had agreed.

The train she'd been waiting twenty minutes for, and the moment that had taken much longer to arrive, was here. The train stopped with a slight squeal of its brakes. The doors opened and two people got off. The man with his newly purchased ticket got on. Robyn stayed where she was.

One of the passengers approached her.

"Happy thirtieth birthday, Mum," Robyn said.

"Does this mean you forgive me for running away?"

"No, Mum. It means I understand why you did and I'm pleased you've come back."

Mother and daughter hugged.

"I'm pleased too, I think," Dad said.

Robyn looked at him standing a little way from them, holding baby Helen. He hadn't stayed quietly in the car, but maybe that was right. It was time for him to speak.

"You only think?" Mum asked.

"My daughters need their mother and I want my wife. Is that woman back?"

"Yes."

"Then I'm pleased."

11. Lest We Forget

Martha balled the tissue in her hand. She'd picked it up intending to wipe Billy's chin with it; a trickle of saliva dribbled from his mouth. She resisted the temptation to dab it away. Billy wasn't a baby and she mustn't treat him as one. If the dribble worried him he could wipe it away with the back of his hand. He often did.

"It's cold out, Billy. I think we'll need hats and gloves as well as our coats."

She helped him into a padded jacket and fastened the zip before pulling on a warm coat for herself.

As she bent to pin on his poppy he whispered, "Ma."

He mumbled other sounds too sometimes, but no clear words. It was her name he was trying to say though. She cleaned and fed him, dressed him and listened as he tried to say 'Ma'. He knew who she was. He must know that.

He'd speak soon, she was sure of it. Maybe he'd manage to greet Jeff, her husband, when he returned.

"Ready?" she asked.

Billy's head moved in what might have been a nod of agreement.

She pushed him down the street and towards the path where the Remembrance parade was to be held. It felt strange that it was just her and Billy this year. It wasn't really just the two of them though. Generations of her family had served in the forces and the memory of her grandfather and father were with her today. Her husband Jeff was with her too in spirit. Jeff was serving as a medic in Afghanistan, safe inside the green zone. Please God he was safe.

Jeff's family too had a long tradition of serving. So had many in this town. A crowd had gathered to remember loved ones and thank many more they'd never met. As Martha got nearer the cenotaph, she saw veterans who'd lost eyes or limbs, and small children, clutching photographs, who'd lost so much more. All wore their poppies. Even without Billy, Martha would not have been alone here.

As the poems and prayers were read, tears flowed down her cheeks. Aged veterans knelt to lay wreaths for those who'd been lost long ago when these old men were young. Cadets knelt to lay wreaths for those who'd given their lives more recently. Parents and husbands and wives bowed their heads; thinking of those who were still at risk, some of whom would soon make the ultimate sacrifice. She wiped her eyes and when children came forward to speak about the daddies they'd never see again, she crouched to wipe Billy's face. It was difficult to tell quite how much he understood.

"Martha, will you and Billy join us for a drink to the regiment?" asked Terry, a man who'd served briefly with Jeff.

Martha hesitated. Could she bear to listen to more talk of fighting and danger? No, they wouldn't say such things in front of her and Billy. The talk would all be of comradeship, shared jokes and remembered friends. She looked down at Billy. He was watching Terry, listening to his words, smiling. Maybe the uniform reminded him of Jeff, maybe his thoughts were elsewhere, but being amongst men from the regiment wasn't going to hurt him.

"Thanks, Terry. We'd like that."

The men poured drinks. Whisky for those who wanted it, juice for those who didn't. Billy's glass had a straw in it and was nestled in the crook of his arm. Jokes were told. Martha managed to laugh, it seemed that Billy did too. They sang the regimental song and Billy's lips moved. She moved close, but couldn't hear his voice over that of the others.

As she pushed him home, she thought of the song. Music helped with language, didn't it? That's why children were taught nursery rhymes. Billy had been trying to sing, she was positive about that. Martha sang again. After the first line, a second voice joined hers. The words weren't clear, perhaps even not words at all, but Billy was singing the tune of the regimental song. She stopped and turned him back towards the cenotaph as they sang the final verse.

Martha crouched down and rested her forehead against Billy's, just for a moment. Billy's gloved hand reached out and covered hers where it rested on the arm of his wheelchair. He mumbled words that might have been, 'thank you, Martha'. It really didn't matter what he actually said. What mattered was how he felt and what he thought.

Billy's drooping mouth might not be able to quite pronounce his daughter-in-law's name, but he knew she was there. He might not yet be able to put into words his thanks for her unstinting care since his stroke, but she didn't mind. Today, she didn't want gratitude. The eleventh of November was the day for her to be grateful.

12. Home And Away

"I've made my mind up, love," George announced as he sat down to breakfast.

"About what?" Mary asked. She hoped he hadn't decided to give up his new passion for healthy eating in the mornings. Pouring fruit juice and opening the box of muesli was much easier than cooking the eggs, bacon and mushrooms he'd previously enjoyed, as well as being much better for them both.

"My retirement money. I've decided what to spend it on." He held up his car keys and tapped the distinctive Mercedes logo on the fob. The fob she'd given him many years ago, because although she knew he loved them, they weren't in a position to buy one of the ridiculously expensive cars it represented.

Mary sighed. She could think of better things to spend the money on than George's delayed mid-life crisis. A nice long holiday for a start. Still, he had earned it and it wasn't as though they strictly needed it for anything else now. George had provided all the money to raise their children and maintain the house throughout their married life. Mary had saved the money she'd received from her various part-time jobs, using it for treats for the family and herself.

"Don't worry, I'll keep back enough for the family trip to Legoland I know you've been hoping to arrange."

He had noticed her subtle hints, then.

"Thanks, dear. The grandchildren will love it."

"Yes, nearly as much as you'll love treating them."

"So, what are you getting? One of those open top, sporty cars with no boot?" She tried to show some enthusiasm, really she did, but she heard it come out as a whinge.

"No, nothing like that. Hardly be practical would it?"

"No." Mary felt bad at imagining George wearing a ponytail and trendy jeans whilst cruising around in a shiny convertible. She knew that wasn't his style.

"Promise me it won't be one of those black ones that look like hearses," she pleaded.

"I promise."

Mary made coffee and reminded herself that he'd worked for it and deserved to treat himself as he'd always put her and the family first.

"Make me one too, would you, love?" George asked.

"You don't want your fresh juice?"

"I'll have both. This muesli takes a bit of washing down."

Bless him, he was doing his best to adjust to the changes she'd suggested for his health. She'd just have to adjust to a change in the future she'd imagined for them. As she poured the coffee Mary supposed she'd rather taken him for granted in the plans for that cash. She'd have liked a holiday and kidded herself that would be a treat for him too. The holiday would, of course, involve a visit to the children; Oliver and his wife in their one-bedroom starter home and Sally with her large family squashed into a bigger, but not big enough for them, house.

George wasn't getting enough of a lump sum to help the children afford larger homes. Mary had no reason to complain, but it'd be nice to see the kids. See them properly not just for an hour or two so whoever had done the driving could get home that night. With a bit of money, she and

George could book into a hotel nearby, perhaps take the kids out for a fancy meal – well fancy for Oliver and his wife, McDonald's or pizza for Sally and her brood.

"Coffee ready, love?" George asked.

"Yes, sorry. I was thinking." She added milk to his drink.

"About our new wheels?"

"Sort of."

"Shall we go to the showroom once we've drunk this?" George asked.

"Showroom? You're getting a new one and blowing all that money in one go?"

George put down his mug and reached for her hand.

"Sorry, George. I didn't mean… " She trailed off, embarrassed that her personal pep talk hadn't done much good.

George rubbed the back of her hand with his thumb. "Actually, I thought second-hand might be better if we can find one in good condition. Be nice to have a bit of money to spend once we got there, wouldn't it?"

"Got where?"

"Wherever we want to go, but knowing you, that'll include plenty of visits to the kids."

Of course it would. He wasn't going to stop driving her to see them just because he'd bought a fancy car. Actually, it might mean they went more often. Mary was sure she could persuade George to agree that some of the money he was keeping back could be used for meals out. Oliver's wife had mentioned a new Italian restaurant near them; she'd like to try that.

Despite getting wet whilst rushing out to the car in the rain, Mary was feeling much more positive by the time she was buckled into the car and they were driving across town.

"So where exactly is this showroom?"

"Just the other side of the junction."

Mary looked across and saw a dealership emblazoned with that distinctive Mercedes logo, and sports cars gleaming on the forecourt. There was a really smart red one. If that was the one George wanted it would certainly give the neighbours something to talk about!

"George, you've missed the turning."

"No, love. I haven't."

He turned off at the last exit and then drove right by a perfectly good car park. Was he going to expect her to walk half a mile in the rain?

"Here we are," George said as he stopped the car.

Mary looked around her in bewilderment. Although the vehicles around her were all of George's favourite make, they weren't cars.

"You're buying a campervan?"

"Yes, I thought a smaller one would be best. We could park it on the driveway when we visit the kids and it'd be easier to get on the ferry if we fancied going away for a nice holiday in the sun."

13. Get A Grip

"Oh b… bother," I shouted out in frustration as I dropped the paintbrush yet again.

Up until halfway through, I'd thought my pregnancy was going to be a doddle. I'd avoided morning sickness, my skin looked radiant and so did my smile. I'd got my chipped tooth fixed for free and my husband believed in my craving for white chocolate truffles and made me a batch every week so I had plenty to smile about. Obviously the baby was the main reason for my happiness, but those truffles are really, really good.

It was all going very well until my wrist started playing up. It hurt – a lot. The worst bit was that I was finding it difficult to grip anything properly. I'd finished sanding the woodwork and stripping the wallpaper in the nursery. Duncan had offered to help but, thanks to my dad, I'm much better at DIY projects than he is. Dad had decorated my nursery before I was born. As a toddler I'd 'helped' him decorate my room and as I got older he'd taught me how to do the work myself. When I explained to Duncan, he'd been happy to let me carry on the tradition.

"I'll go and put dinner on then. Just promise you'll call me if you need to move anything and promise you'll be very careful on the stepladders."

I'd agreed, even though I personally felt it would have been easier to move the steps myself than to keep going downstairs to ask him. Now I'd done all the hard work and couldn't seem to do the fun bit; the painting. I was making a complete mess of it.

Thinking back to the decorating lessons Dad had given me, I knew the only thing I was doing wrong was to hold the brush incorrectly. Maybe Dad could give me some tips on ways to reduce the pain without taking painkillers. He'd done so much decorating that he must have got an achy wrist at times. I gave him a call and explained the problem.

"What have you been doing with yourself, Kaz?" Dad demanded. "You should be taking it easy in your condition."

"Dad, I'm fine really. Duncan is taking great care of me. Anyway, the doctor said it was best to keep active. All I've been doing is sanding the woodwork and… "

"Sounds like carpal tunnel syndrome to me," he interrupted.

"What's that?"

"Basically it's a place in your wrist where one bit swells up and squashes a nerve and that hurts."

"Like me and Duncan sitting on the sofa – as I grow bigger, he complains he's getting squashed?"

"Yes. Hopefully you're not squashing him enough to cause pain and numbness, but with your big bum, I wouldn't be surprised."

"Oi! Cheeky." I should have known sympathy from Dad wouldn't last long. He does care, but he'd rather people got on with things than made a fuss. "He only says it when he wants me to get up and make him a cup of tea. He reckons it's good for my circulation," I complained.

Dad and I both knew it wasn't a fair complaint as I could rarely sit still for long and Duncan never expected me to wait on him.

Dad laughed. "Good man. You'd best go make him one

now if you can remember where the kitchen is. Don't stir it though, that'll hurt your wrist. Oh and get yourself down the doctor and see what he can do for you."

His last words didn't reassure me much. If Dad was suggesting seeing a doctor he must really think I had something wrong.

After listening to my symptoms and examining my wrist, the doctor said, "I'm sure this is carpal tunnel syndrome. For some reason it does occasionally occur during pregnancy."

"So it's nothing to do with the decorating? Just something that's come up because I'm pregnant?"

"It could be due to either of those things. We won't know until after you give birth."

The doctor explained what caused carpal tunnel and the different treatments available. I began to panic.

"I can't grip things properly, how will I be able to hold my baby?"

"If we can relieve the pain then you should soon be able to do everything you could before."

"I can't take painkillers though, not while I'm pregnant."

"There are some that are safe, but a splint might be a better option. Try using one and resting that arm and we'll see how you get on."

He gave me a prescription for a splint and I was lucky that the pharmacy already had one in the right size. I felt a bit silly with the pink plastic contraption Velcroed around my hand and arm but it did feel very supportive.

I did as the doctor advised, much to Duncan's relief. He seemed to like being the capable one for a change. When the kitchen sink blocked up I didn't immediately rush to the garage for my tool kit or even call Dad when Duncan told me about the problem. An hour later the water was running freely down the plughole. Duncan did have a chat with Dad during that time, but maybe he only called him to report on the improvement to my wrist.

Duncan fussed around me and cooked all my favourite foods to cheer me up. He knew that sitting still whilst there was work to be done made me edgy.

The pain in my wrist eased off considerably after just a few days. My hand ached a little, especially first thing in the morning but it wasn't too bad. The painting all got done although it took longer than I'd expected. The nursery was perfect by the time Charlotte was born. I'm completely free of pain now, which is just as well as my new daughter is a right handful!

Dad says she's going to be just like me and has already bought her first tool box. Duncan thinks she'll be just like me too, but says he's going to get her an apron and cookbooks just in case he's wrong. I hope he is and she helps him to make me those white chocolate truffles every Mother's Day.

14. Age Related Problems

"Don't be so childish, Serena," Mum snapped.

I sulked. Yeah, I know sulking is childish too, but life wasn't fair and other than screaming and shouting, I couldn't think of anything else to do. Yesterday, I'd asked Mum if it was OK for me to stay out late on Friday night. I thought it was bound to be OK because I didn't have school the next day and I'd be going to a public place with a responsible adult. Any reasonable person would think it's OK for a thirteen-year-old girl to go to the pictures under such circumstances. It wasn't a horror picture or anything X-rated, just a nice romantic comedy. Mum went ballistic. I should know better apparently. I don't know what she's got against Tommy. He's nineteen and has a job and drives a car and is just lovely, but she wouldn't let me go. I'm too young. Huh.

Today, on the way home from school I saw a beautiful dress in the window of a bridal shop. Gorgeous it is, full and frilly in the skirt, but with a fitted bodice and dainty little straps. The peach colour would really show off my dark hair and blue eyes.

"No." That's what Mum said when I asked her to buy it for me.

"But, Mum it's lovely and I've never been a bridesmaid and… " I could see I wasn't getting through to her, so I pointed out that my older sister had just been bought a dress that cost twice as much for her school prom.

"Yes, but she's finishing school this year and you're not."

Too young again, you see. I cried like the baby she seems

to think I am until she told me not to be childish. So then I went to my room and sulked.

Mum came up after a while and gave me a hug. "Sorry, love. I've got a lot on my mind and I didn't mean to snap."

I hadn't meant to act like a spoilt kid either, but she's the grown-up and the one who should know better.

"There's nothing wrong with wanting a pretty dress, whatever your age, but I just can't afford to buy it for you right now."

Well, why hadn't she just explained?

"Are you worried about money, Mum?" I asked. "I could get a paper round or something... "

She hugged me again. "Don't worry, love."

"I might be too young for dates, but I do know about the credit crunch," I told her to show how grown up I am.

"It's not that."

"What's worrying you, then?"

She waited a while before answering, as if she was trying to decide what to say. "Your grandad for one thing."

"He's not ill?" I was worried. I remember, just about, how awful it was when Granny died. I really was a little kid then, but not so young I don't remember everyone crying.

"He seems a bit confused. He was asking me something about bridesmaid dresses today. Heaven only knows what he was thinking about."

That explained Mum not wanting to talk to me about the same thing. I didn't like the idea that he might be going senile, but wasn't too bothered as it seemed so unlikely. Grandad is sharp and clever; he looks ancient, but you forget that as soon as he speaks.

"Shall I go round and see how he is?" I offered.

Mum was pleased with that idea and sent me round there with a big slab of ginger cake as though he was a kid getting a treat from a grandparent or as though his mind was already gone and he might be forgetting to eat. Maybe she didn't mean it either of those ways and just wanted to get rid of some of it – she's been making loads of it lately.

When I got to Grandad's house, his girlfriend Minnie was there. Don't let on to Mum that I've told you she's his girlfriend, because she acted very odd when I asked her about that. Said it was only teenagers who have boyfriend and girlfriends and the novelty soon wore off. Dad didn't seem keen on the subject either.

Grandad put the kettle on and Minnie told me how pretty I am and how she thought it was a shame I always hid myself in trousers and baggy jumpers. When I told her about the pretty dress I wasn't allowed, she started to laugh. I knew she wasn't being nasty, but I couldn't see what she thought was funny. Grandad could and laughed so much I had to take the tray of tea and Mum's cake from him.

I asked them what they'd been doing and they said they'd been sightseeing. They get free bus travel, so spend sunny days going to all the towns that are in travelling distance and pretend to be tourists.

"We can take our time to look round at all the interesting buildings and little parks that busy people who are working or shopping hardly notice," Minnie explained.

"Not feeling you've got to rush about all the time is one of the perks to being old," Grandad said.

"Glad there's an age that has perks," I grumbled telling them about my arguments with Mum and how Dad was working overtime so there wasn't anyone to hear my side of the story.

"You've got us, love," he said.

"Thanks," I said and squeezed his hand.

Grandad and Minnie pulled faces at each other and I knew something was up and they couldn't decide who should tell me. Grandad kept nodding at Minnie.

"You tell her," Minnie said, which I thought was a lot more sensible than Grandad's crazy nodding.

"I've asked Minnie to marry me," he said.

"Brilliant! Er, you did say yes?"

"I did," Minnie confirmed.

"We have you to thank," Grandad told me. "I don't know if you remember, but you called Minnie my girlfriend once and got quite a reaction."

"Yeah."

"I realised you were right and that's exactly how I feel about her and plucked up the courage to ask if she felt the same way."

"Come on, Grandad. That was obvious! I knew that, especially when you told me you knew each other years ago, before you met Granny."

"It wasn't anything romantic then. I was a schoolgirl and your grandad drove the school bus."

"So is there a big difference in your ages?"

"Twelve years. It doesn't seem so much now, but it is when you're fourteen," Minnie told me.

I nodded. Six years is a lot too, when you're thirteen and the boy who asked you out is nineteen.

Minnie said, "I have something to ask you. If you don't think you're too old for it, would you be my bridesmaid?"

"I will. I'd love it – even if I don't get to choose the dress."

"You can choose," Grandad said. "On one condition; you help us break the news to your mother."

I agreed, but as it happens, I got off pretty lightly there. The phone rang. Grandad answered.

"Hello, love… Yes… Of course… Nothing wrong, is there?… Everyone?… Yes."

"That was your mother. She's asked me to bring you home as she wants a family chat."

We all went back home, Minnie too as they decided it wasn't fair to ask me to keep their secret and the family chat was a good opportunity to share their news.

There was more tea and ginger cake as we all sat around the kitchen table.

"I don't quite know where to start… " Mum said. She looked at Dad and he did that nodding thing that Grandad had been doing earlier.

"The family is going to get bigger… " she said and gave a sweet funny smile.

"Fantastic!" I said, glad I didn't have to try to do any talking her round.

"How?" my sister asked.

"I… we… "

"Your mum and I are going to have another baby," Dad told us.

I was glad I'd already said 'fantastic' as I couldn't speak at all.

"But how?" my sister asked. I thought she was old enough to know the answer to that one.

Mum giggled and said it was my fault. I knew she was old

enough to know it doesn't work like that.

"We'd been having a difficult time," Dad said. He and Mum explained things hadn't been good between them until something I said got them talking and they realised they didn't want things to be over. They shut up then which I was pleased about because there's such a thing as too much information.

"Congratulations," Minnie said, ever so quietly, and suddenly it was all OK. My sister hugged Mum, then I did and Grandad shook Dad's hand.

Minnie and Grandad started up the nodding again. I didn't think I could sit through it the third time.

"Grandad and Minnie are getting married," I blurted out. There was silence. "I'm going to be a big sister and a bridesmaid – how cool is that?"

Pretty cool as it turned out. I looked fabulous as Minnie's bridesmaid and just as great the week afterwards when I wore the dress again when I was godmother to my baby sister. I got to eat loads of cake on both occasions, which is one of the perks of being a kid.

15. Sunday Roast

"Good news, everyone can make it for the twenty-third," Allen said as he put the phone down.

"Good," Wendy said, attempting a smile.

"What's up? I haven't got the day wrong, have I?"

"No, it's fine. I'm just thinking about what to feed them."

"Just cook one of your smashing Sunday roasts, everyone will like that."

Wendy nodded, but had her doubts. Allen loved her roast beef, Yorkshire puddings and apple pie; unfortunately his family didn't share his simple tastes. It would be too dull for them. Not that they'd say anything, they'd all thank her politely and eat a little of whatever she served.

Allen's mother, a former gourmet chef, had passed her love of fine food to her family. Wendy loved the meals she was offered at family dinner parties; delicate creamy Italian dishes, aromatic Thai food, exquisite French creations, the list seemed endless.

As newlyweds, Wendy and Allen had been invited to dinners at his parents' home and then with each of his three sisters in turn. Every evening had been a success. Wendy felt too intimidated by their culinary skills to host her own dinner party; instead she and Allen took the whole family out for lunch. That had been only partially successful; Wendy had felt guilty when the others insisted on paying for their share.

"It doesn't matter who pays for the food, Wendy dear," her mother-in-law had said. "What's important is that we get together and enjoy each other's company."

Everyone else agreed with her, saying that by making the booking Wendy had taken her turn at providing a family meal.

"Besides, this has been a pleasant change from our usual dinner parties," Sonia had added.

After the lunch, the whole family had gone for a walk together. It had been fun to spend time relaxing with the family rather than worrying about which fork to use. Wendy's own family was small and far away, so she was delighted to get to know her in-laws.

The next time Wendy and Allen provided a meal, it had been the height of summer just after they'd finished landscaping the garden. Using that excuse, Wendy suggested a barbecue. Again she'd felt a bit of a cheat as she hadn't cooked a thing. All the men had wanted a go and those who weren't turning sizzling steaks and succulent chicken had chopped vegetables, tossed salads and buttered crispy bread. Everyone was having such an enjoyable day she realised it really didn't matter who did what.

Since then, Wendy and Allen had been to dinner at the homes of all the others and it was their turn again. Wendy considered hiring caterers, but knew she'd feel a terrible fraud; besides someone was bound to ask about the ingredients and she'd be caught out. It was better to be considered a poor cook than a liar. If only she knew how to cook something other than boring old roasts, unimaginative hot-pots and predictable pies.

Her sisters-in-law must have sensed her unease. They each, separately, offered help and suggestions for making things less daunting.

Sonia had rung first. "You don't have to do a five course

meal, Wendy. We know how busy you are at work and wouldn't want you to use all your free time cooking for us."

"It doesn't have to be dinner, Wendy," Rachel had said. "If a weekend lunch would suit you better, that will be fine with everyone."

Allen had praised her Sunday lunch, so it looked as though that's what it would have to be. She reminded herself they wouldn't stop liking her even if they weren't fond of her cooking. Her father-in-law might well appreciate it, she supposed. She'd heard him mutter, "Nothing wrong with decent British grub," on more than one occasion.

No amount of home-made horseradish sauce and rich gravy would make such an ordinary meal exciting enough for Allen's older sister, Sonia though. She favoured interesting touches, such as raspberry vinegar, pomegranate seeds or walnut oil to give her dishes individuality. Sonia's food was always so beautifully presented Wendy felt it should be photographed, rather than damaged with cutlery. Admiring course after course of intricate creations was a real pleasure for Wendy, although it seemed a shame that Sonia spent so much of the evening in the kitchen applying finishing touches. Conversation was difficult as people waited for her to come back or repeated whatever had been said in her absence.

Choosing the choicest cut of prime Irish beef and the freshest and tastiest of vegetables wouldn't impress Rachel. She preferred exotic ingredients sourced from around the world. Eastern spices, tropical fruits and rare nuts often featured in her menus. The effort she put into locating unusual and authentic items was rewarded by the most mouth-watering aromas and flavours. Almost every component of every meal had been a new and delightful experience for Wendy. Unfortunately Rachel seldom seemed to enjoy her own cooking. After tasting, adjusting seasoning and tasting again to ensure each dish was perfectly balanced she rarely had much appetite left.

Lynda would approve her choice of local food and organic vegetables at least. Wendy's vegetarian sister-in-law clearly wouldn't eat the beef though; a suitable alternative would have to be prepared.

The men seemed easier to please. As long as they had enough food on their plates and a decent glass of wine to go with it, she'd never heard a word of criticism from them.

To be fair, she'd never heard the women complain either and knew they wouldn't do it to her. It was more the slight air of competition with which they announced each dish and the feeling Wendy could never match their standards that worried her. After talking her concerns over with Allen, Wendy decided not to try anything elaborate. Cooking for such a large group would be challenging enough, without attempting a recipe she was unsure of.

An hour before the family where due, Wendy took stock. Allen was in the dining room; arranging borrowed chairs, polishing cutlery and generally doing what he could to help. The meat was almost done and smelling wonderful. It would soon be time to take it out and allow it to rest, so it would carve perfectly.

The baby carrots, Savoy cabbage and runner beans were prepared ready for cooking. A large pan of red wine gravy was ready on the side and the batter mix for the Yorkshire puddings was in the fridge. The brown sugar topped apple pie was ready to be put into the warm oven whilst they ate the first course.

The roasted vegetables; parsnips, cubes of squash and

potatoes were already crisping and looked set to be a triumph. Wendy had even remembered to cook some in a separate dish without meat juices for Lynda.

No! Wendy had forgotten about a main course for Lynda. She couldn't possibly be expected to eat beef. Wendy tried to recall the main courses Lynda had served or eaten at other people's houses. It was no use; she wouldn't know how to cook them even if she'd had the ingredients. The only experience Wendy had of vegetarian cooking was making cheese omelettes and macaroni cheese for a college friend. She'd have to make something with cheese. There was a large piece of Stilton in the fridge; Wendy was intending to serve a cheeseboard as a foolproof way of adding an extra course to the lunch. She'd already checked the cheeses were all suitable for vegetarians.

Wendy poured herself a glass of wine from the bottle she'd opened to make the gravy and gulped some down.

"Calming your nerves?" Allen asked.

"It'll take more than wine. You'll never believe how stupid I've been."

"You're not stupid and I find it hard to believe you've made a mistake. You even checked the custard was suitable for vegetarians."

"Custard, yes. And the cheese, almost everything."

"What are you giving Lynda, anyway? You never said."

"Guess why not," Wendy said.

"Because it's a surprise?"

"It certainly will be."

"Well, as you're holding a block of Stilton, I'm guessing it's Stilton surprise."

"Keep going," Wendy said, willing him to realise what

was wrong. It might not seem so bad if he guessed.

"I don't know what all the fancy things are called," he said. "What's the proper name for roast Stilton surprise with Yorkshire pudding?"

"Allen, you're a genius," Wendy said, handing him her wine glass. "Here, you drink this; I've got some creative cookery to do."

Wendy whisked up some more batter, chopped stilton and buttered an ovenproof dish. Just before her guests were due to arrive, she poured batter into the dish, dropped in the cheese and put it in the oven, next to the bun tin for individual Yorkshires, with the heat turned high. Wendy was switching on the heat under the vegetable steamer as the first car pull into the drive.

"Is there anything I can do?" Allen's mother asked.

"No, thank you; it's all under control." It felt good to be able to say that. "Come and sit down and I'll bring you a drink."

Wendy greeted each of her guests and joined them for a drink, confident that she'd already done everything she could to ensure the meal was successful. Her sisters-in-law offered assistance and praised her for her organisational skills as she assured them all she needed to do was put the vegetables into serving dishes.

"I'll just check how they're doing," she said.

Wendy didn't want any of them in the kitchen. If the Yorkshire puddings were flat or the runner beans had turned to mush, she planned to keep them well out of sight. It didn't take long to put the food into appropriate dishes as she wasn't bothering with fancy glazes or chopped parsley. She didn't dare look at the Stilton Surprise as she removed the well risen Yorkshire puddings and, very gently, closed the oven door.

"If you'd all like to go through to the dining room… Allen, could you help carry things?"

Straining gravy into the jug to remove the lumps reminded her there was no sauce for the Stilton Surprise. There was the remains of a jar of cranberry sauce in the fridge, perhaps that would do? Wendy scraped it into a dish and stirred in marmalade and orange juice to make it go further. Heaven knows what it would taste like, but it looked rather pretty. Allen took the dish from her along with the last of the vegetables.

Wendy pulled on her oven mitts and opened the door. She slid in the apple pie and removed the Surprise. It looked quite good. It smelled really good. She carried it in and placed it in front of Lynda.

"A soufflé? Oh how lovely. It smells like blue cheese."

"Stilton," Allen said. "It's Wendy's own recipe."

Allen carved the beef and everyone helped themselves to small portions of vegetables, Yorkshires and gravy. There were several comments about how nice it all looked and how wonderful it smelled. Then they began to eat.

Wendy tasted her food. The beef wasn't tough, the vegetables weren't mush, the carefully strained gravy wasn't lumpy; it was an ordinary Sunday lunch, just as she often cooked. The family all complimented her very nicely, as she'd expected they would. Then they acted less predictably.

"Can I try your soufflé, Lynda?" Rachel asked.

"No. You'll have to wait until you come to mine. I'm going to get the recipe from Wendy and make this myself. You will share the recipe with me? And for the sauce?"

"Yes, if you like. It's really very simple… "

"Simply delicious, that's what it is."

"Allen, carve us another slice of beef, will you?" his father asked.

"And for me."

"Me too."

Each of the men asked for more, as did Rachel and her mother. Everyone ate until there was nothing more than the end of the beef and some cabbage left. That didn't prevent everyone from eating a slice of apple pie, topped with creamy custard.

Before her guests left, they made Wendy promise that whenever it was 'her turn' to cook, she'd make a Sunday Roast.

"Roast pork next time," Allen said. "Wendy does a lovely bit of crackling."

Allen's parents were last to leave. His mother came into the kitchen, carrying the empty pie plate and custard jug.

"That was an excellent meal, Wendy."

"It was just an ordinary… "

"I was a professional chef. I know good cooking when I taste it. Getting the simple things right is often the most troublesome."

"It's kind of you to say so… " She trailed off as an item on the work surface caught her attention. Wendy began to chuckle.

"I'm not just being polite, my dear. Everything was just perfect."

As Wendy gazed at the tub of neatly prepared, still raw, Brussels sprouts, she couldn't control her laughter.

Her mother-in-law looked to see what had amused her.

She picked up the sprouts. "When you came to dinner last time, I'd planned to decorate the starters with sliced quails eggs. I cooked them, put them in cold water and forgot about them until I went to the kitchen with the empty plates. Lynda once bought champagne which she found under the car seat two days later and… I won't go on. We all do it. I'm so glad you really are one of us."

16. Slipping Through Her Fingers

Vicky sighed with relief when her daughter, Alison, came out to help carry in the shopping and put it away. As usual on a Monday, Vicky had collected her elderly neighbour and taken the lady to the supermarket after work. She was a dear soul, Mrs Andrews, but made the simple trip into something of an endurance test.

Once the food was stowed away, Vicky poured herself a glass of wine. She almost made the mistake of offering Alison a Coke but stopped just in time. Last time she'd done that her daughter accused Vicky of treating her like a kid. Vicky had quite enough on her mind with her mum being in hospital. Vicky was having difficulty arranging transport for the physio her mother would need after the knee replacement operation and working out how she could fit caring for her around work shifts and family life. She could do without the added drama of an argument. Vicky, guessing her daughter wouldn't like dry red wine, did what she could to keep the peace and offered Alison a glass of sweet sherry.

"What? Why are you treating me like Gran?"

"Would that really be so bad?" Vicky asked, sharply. Too sharply.

"Being like Gran wouldn't be so bad, no. Being treated the way you treat her would."

Vicky gasped as though Alison had slapped her. "You hardly know her other than for the cheques she sends you on birthdays and at Christmas. I'm the one that worries about her and about you."

While Vicky ranted, Alison poured her own glass of wine. "Mum, I keep telling you, you don't have to worry about Gran or me, I'm fine."

"Oh really? So, I'm wasting my time getting up early to take you to school?"

"Work, Mum. I work now, remember?"

"That was a slip of the tongue," Vicky said almost truthfully. It was hard thinking of her little girl being nineteen and working for a living.

"Mum, I really appreciate you taking me in, especially when the weather's bad, but you don't have to if it's inconvenient."

It was true, Alison had repeatedly said she could go by bus but Vicky worried about her on her own, especially when she worked late. Perhaps, Vicky thought, her own job as a special constable made her extra cautious. She did tend to see the results of the worst things that could happen and had to remind herself they were rare occurrences. Alison was a sensible girl. She often got herself to and from the badminton club they both attended, when Vicky's job meant she had to skip a session.

"Sorry," Vicky muttered. "I guess I'm just tired."

"I know you are, Mum." Alison gave her a hug. "Don't worry so much. Gran's fine. A knee replacement is pretty routine these days and she's got plenty of friends popping in to see her."

After Vicky dropped Alison at work the following day she vacuumed the house and took down the spare room curtains to wash them. Before she got them in the washing machine, she'd come to her senses. She should have been in the hospital visiting her mum, not making work for herself. She should have gone before but she had been scared to. She didn't like to think of her mum being ill and in hospital. But Alison was right, her gran, Vicky's mother, wasn't ill.

Outside the hospital, Vicky nearly lost her nerve and didn't go in. Then she fretted she hadn't brought anything with her. She did realise going off in search of a florist would have been a delaying tactic and knew she'd delayed enough already.

Her mother's ward seemed more like a party venue. There were balloons and cards and people laughing. Right in the centre of everything was Mum. Vicky listened as her mother read a slightly rude and extremely funny poem. Her audience cheered when she reached the end. Mum looked up and saw Vicky staring.

"Vicky, darling! How lovely of you to come. Everyone, this is my wonderful daughter, Vicky."

Mum's friends all greeted her warmly.

"Hi," Vicky said and mumbled about the lack of flowers.

"Not your fault, darling. Silly so-and-sos won't let anyone bring them in, in case they carry the dreaded lurgy. Doesn't matter though. It's you, not some wilted carnations, I'm pleased to see."

Mum was right. She so often was. Mum had said not to worry about her and that she'd be just fine. She should have listened.

Mum's friends were a lot of fun, laughing and joking. Vicky couldn't remember meeting any of them before, so when they eventually left, asked who they were.

"They're all from my poetry group."

"Poetry group!" Vicky had no idea her mum was interested in poetry. She hardly knew anything about her, other than she kept a chain on the door, didn't go out alone after dark and remembered to eat regularly. Those were the only kinds of things Vicky ever discussed with her.

"It's time for my walk," Mum announced.

"Shall I fetch a frame, or will you hold my arm?"

"No! Now don't fuss, Vicky."

Mum walked down the corridor to meet Alison, who'd turned up to visit in her lunch break. She'd been coming every day and it was she who'd written the poem Mum read out. Did Vicky know her own family at all?

"I'm glad you're here to see how well I'm recovering," Mum told Vicky. "It's lovely of you to offer to have me to stay, but I really would be happier at home and it would be so much easier for me to just catch the bus for my physio than for you have to drive me all that way and find a parking space. And you're so busy, darling. It wouldn't be convenient for you."

"All right, Mum, but Alison and I will visit often. Perhaps the three of us can have a nice chat over a drink?"

"Lovely, if you aren't too busy," Mum said. "But don't bring any of that ghastly sherry. I'll mix us up a batch of cocktails."

It was true, Vicky was busy, but she vowed that from then on she wouldn't be too busy to get to know her own family.

17. In The Pink

I'd thought I'd heard a thud as I ran more hot water into my bath, but told myself it was just air in the plumbing. Ignoring the sound of someone walking down the hallway wasn't so easy. Half an hour's relaxation was undone in an instant. Every muscle in my body tensed. There was only one person it could be.

I was annoyed, but not at all surprised my sister Jo had let herself in to my flat without bothering to knock and barged into the bathroom as I'd been trying to enjoy a few quiet minutes of 'me time'. She often does stuff like that.

"What you lazing about in there for? Power cut's over, you'd better get out now or you'll turn into a prune," she said as she threw me a candy-floss coloured towel.

There'd been no power cut of course, I'd lit rose scented candles positioned around my flat to help me relax. Next time I buy something with that in mind, I'll make it a padlock.

"Wow, Susan! I just love what you've done with this place!" Jo said as she followed me into the bedroom.

I was so shocked I dropped my towel and sank onto the paler, but toning quilt. Retrieving the towel from the raspberry crush rug, I began drying my wrinkled skin. Maybe Jo was right that I'd been soaking for long enough.

Annoyingly, she usually is right. As she examined my attempts at brightening my living space, I studied her. Her hair was as glossy as the deep mulberry coloured vase which I'd filled with matching flowers. Her shoes were polished to a sheen my woven throw-covered furniture would never know and unlike my rugs, her silk dress was wrinkle free. I knew I'd never look as elegant as my sister, but as she thought my standard look was 'minimum-effort dishevelled', other than the disadvantage of being damp and naked, I probably didn't look any worse than usual.

Pulling on my marshmallow tinted dressing gown, I began combing my hair and braced myself for her reaction to that. At least I'd kept my hair out the bath, so didn't have cold water dripping down my back.

Jo took the comb from me and inspected my head. "You've changed your hair. It suits you."

This second compliment had me falling back onto the bed. Her noticing wasn't a shock; Jo notices everything. If my nail varnish was chipped, or the floor needed a polish, she didn't hesitate to mention it. Her tastefully made up face, designer clothes and four bedroom house was always immaculate. The same couldn't be said of my coat of mascara, charity shop bargains and studio flat. What was so amazing was my sister saying something nice and not even sounding sarcastic. She never did that.

"Glad you like it," I muttered. I could have told her the truth, but I didn't want to spoil the moment.

For years, Jo had belittled my taste in just about anything. Actually, that's probably not quite fair; she had high standards and wanted me to reach them. Jo is fourteen years older and has always tried to set a good example. She wanted what's best for me; unfortunately she couldn't see that wasn't the same as what was best for her and tended to bully me into trying to improve.

I should have learnt there's no pleasing her, yet still I'd occasionally made an effort to win my big sister's approval.

At last it seemed I'd managed to earn it – by sheer incompetence!

It had started when Jo (rightly) pointed out that my hair was a mess. It's naturally a dull brown, but the sun had lightened the ends, making it look as though it'd been bleached and was growing out, so I'd coloured it. I'd used a lot of dye attempting to even out the tone. Too much; then panicked and washed it out too soon. The result was deep burgundy hair with pink ends.

In my haste, I'd got dye all over the bathroom. I mopped up the mess with a towel and threw it in the wash along with the quilt cover, pillow cases and cushions already in the machine. Everything came out different shades of pink! So did the dressing gown and canvas rugs that I'd dripped dye onto. I'll know better next time – but Jo never will.

18. Mixed Doubles

Paula tapped her fingers impatiently on the work-top as she waited for the microwave to finish. She wanted to dish up tea before the local news came on so she could see if that poor young woman had found her mother's wedding ring. Paula really hoped so. The woman's parents had clearly enjoyed a happy marriage and the daughter sounded as though she'd been very close to them. There wasn't enough of that kind of thing about and Paula hated to think the symbol of it had been lost.

A beep told her the food was ready. She ripped the film tops off their usual Friday night fish pies, slid the dishes onto the waiting trays and carried them into the living room.

"Thanks, love," her husband mumbled as she placed his food next to the jigsaw he was working on.

She sat down with her own tray on her lap just in time to see the reporter standing outside the charity shop, giving the good news. Paula smiled as the girl thanked everyone for their help. It was lovely to see a happy ending. She was still smiling as she took the apple pie from its pack and stirred boiling water onto instant custard.

Her smile faded when she returned to the living room to discover the TV was off and the remote missing from its usual position on the arm of her chair. What was Ian thinking? If she wasn't careful she might miss the start of her soap and then she'd never find out who was responsible for that fire. There wasn't likely to be a happy ending there, but that was life for you and if she didn't watch this episode it'd take her ages to catch up next week. Ah, the remote was on the coffee table, panic over. Paula pressed the button.

"For goodness' sake, can't you turn that thing off occasionally?" Ian asked.

"Why should I? You don't pay any attention to me. I suppose you'll be going down the pub as soon as you've eaten?"

"If you're going to watch soaps all night, I might as well."

Paula turned up the volume to drown out his excuses. He was always off playing darts for the Green Swan's mixed doubles team these days. Funny that; he hadn't gone half as often when they'd only had men's teams.

Ian hadn't had a mobile phone in those days either. Paula turned the volume down again and asked him about it.

"I told you, it's just in case of emergencies and to talk to the kids."

"What emergencies? And the kids hardly ever phone."

"You could call them?"

"Huh!"

She did sometimes but they never had much to say. They hardly ever visited and didn't stay long. No one talked to her much these days. It was a good job she had the TV.

Ian finished his meal and pecked her on the cheek. "Don't wait up. I'm dropping my, er, team-mate off."

Paula wondered if he meant the lady from mixed doubles. She was still wondering about that when the phone rang.

"Hello, is that Mrs Proctor?"

"Yes, but we already have double glazing and aren't interested in that PPP whatsit."

"I'm not selling anything, I'm on the same darts team as

your husband and wondered if he could come down the Green Swan for a practice tonight? We need to do it every week or we'll never beat The Rose and Crown."

Paula almost said he was on his way, but she was starting to have doubts about that. She'd thought he'd been at practice sessions on Monday and Wednesday, but this man didn't sound as though he'd seen Ian. Somehow she managed to stutter, "I think he'll be in later," before sinking into her armchair, a worried frown on her face.

Perhaps the caller had made a mistake. Paula didn't know him, or how well he knew Ian. She didn't know any of his darts friends. Ian used to ask her to come and support him at matches. She never went and he never asked her now. Paula was still thinking about why he no longer wanted her there when her son and daughter-in-law arrived unexpectedly.

The couple seemed ill at ease and whispered to each other more than they spoke to her.

Paula couldn't quite catch the conversation over the TV, but was sure her son's wife said something like, "No wonder your dad is carrying on like he is."

"What was that?'" she asked.

"Oh, nothing."

Not much change there. They never really talked to her when they visited. They'd chat to Ian in the kitchen as he made them a cup of tea, then sit on her sofa talking to each other. It didn't matter, she'd heard enough to understand Ian was up to something and Paula was the last to know.

When Ian arrived home that night, all the decent shows had long since finished and Paula was in bed. She decided not to tackle him until the morning when they could talk properly. Somehow though, she never seemed to find the right moment. Perhaps confrontation wasn't the answer.

On Saturday evening, when Ian carried the finished tea things back into the kitchen before going to the pub, Paula turned off the television.

Ian rushed back. "Is it broken?"

"No, I'm coming with you."

"You're doing what? Isn't it EastEnders or Neighbours or something?" He seemed flustered.

"Yes, I'll have to record it."

"Oh, right."

"It is all right for me to come?" Paula asked.

"Yes, lovely."

Ian's darts friends all greeted her pleasantly, even his doubles partner. Although that slim young redhead wouldn't meet Paula's eyes she didn't show Ian any particular attention either. Maybe she wasn't the problem?

Paula went to more matches. She chose different nights so as not to disrupt her viewing too much and so Ian could never be sure when she'd attend. Occasionally she was sure he sent a text message just before they went out, but Ian always acted as though her company was a pleasant surprise. They never gave anyone a lift home.

Occasionally their son and his wife joined her at the pub to watch Ian play. Sue, her daughter-in-law, always asked what Paula had been up to.

"Oh you know, the usual. How about you?"

"I finished that bookmark I was telling you about."

What was the girl on about, did she mean she'd read a book? "Oh, did you enjoy it?"

"Yes and it looked really pretty. I've decided to be a bit more adventurous for my next project and work a cushion cover."

Oh, embroidery! Paula used to love embroidery. The chatted about the stitches and colours Sue planned to use, then progressed to a really easy recipe Sue had discovered for chocolate cookies and the new silicone muffin tray she'd bought. Paula used to love baking.

She couldn't think why she'd given up her hobbies. She also couldn't think why she'd never got on with Sue, or why the young woman never spoke to Paula at the house.

Sue suggested they enrolled in an evening class for appliqué work.

"Tuesday isn't a good night. There's a programme I always watch on at the same time."

"You could always record it," Sue suggested.

"Yes, I suppose so." It occurred to Paula that she'd recorded several programmes recently. She hadn't watched any of them back and couldn't honestly say she felt she'd missed very much. How odd.

Paula enjoyed her evening classes. She was concerned she was making a mistake by providing a regular occasion when she was out the way and wouldn't know what Ian was up to, but she couldn't allow her suspicions to rule her life. She started baking more frequently too.

"Oh, lovely!" Ian said when Paula carried in a plate of cakes. "Put them there, love. I don't want to get crumbs on your embroidery."

She in turn was careful not to allow her silks and patches to spill over onto his jigsaws. Working quietly side by side, they talked to each other about the kids, his job and planned a holiday. Ian seemed interested in her again. Paula couldn't think why they'd ever stopped having these sorts of conversations. Hopefully he'd not really been having an affair, but if he had, surely it was over now?

Paula was just dishing up home-made steak pie and fresh vegetables when Ian called into the kitchen.

"Let's have our tea on trays tonight."

Although she wondered why he'd made the request, she did as he asked. Just a few weeks ago a tray in front of the TV was normal, so why was she reluctant to miss sitting opposite her husband and hearing about his plans for sorting out the front garden?

Paula was even more disappointed when she carried in the meal and Ian switched on the television. It seemed like an excuse to ignore her. Had he felt that way when she watched soaps all evening and didn't hear a word he said? No wonder he'd been more interested in the charms of his darts partner.

They watched a news report of a girl who met her soon to be husband through darts matches. Paula had never seen the boy before, but the slender redhead looked familiar.

"Isn't that your… " she started to say.

"Shhh, I want to listen to this," Ian interrupted.

"Your love of darts has led to boyfriend trouble in the past, I understand," the interviewer asked the girl.

"That's right," she agreed. "I'm a bit fanatical about it and couldn't possibly have a husband who doesn't feel the same way."

"But luckily you met Darren Jones in the pub where you were playing with your team-mate," he glanced at his notes. "Ian Proctor."

"That's right. Darren said if we won, he'd buy me a drink. Luckily we did and things went from there."

"Until you asked him to prove his devotion to the game as

well as to you?"

"Yes. I said I wouldn't marry him unless he could beat me."

The boy never said a word, but he grinned and nodded agreement with everything the red head said.

"And that's where Mr Proctor came to the rescue?" the interviewer prompted.

"Yes, that's right. He taught Darren to play and he did beat me. Only just, mind. Since then we've played in a couple of competitions together and won some money towards our honeymoon. Thanks, Ian." She blew a kiss at the screen.

Darren held up a small trophy and a set of darts. "Yeah, thanks, Ian."

The television showed a clip of the couple playing darts.

"That was you teaching him," Paula said.

Ian nodded.

"That's why you weren't practising with the team?"

"Yes."

"But I thought… "

"I was having an affair?"

"Well, yes," Paula admitted.

"I know you did. Sorry but it was the only way I could think of to get you away from the TV. I was so worried about you not going out or taking any interest in anything. Even when the kids visited you were more interested in TV than in them. We never did anything together any more, I thought it'd be good for us to go out occasionally."

"Hmm, and watching you play darts is your idea of doing something together is it?" she asked.

"I thought it was a start. We can do other things, have a

meal out or watch the pictures, whatever you like."

"I've got a better idea. Teach me to play darts. Looks like you'll be needing a new doubles partner."

"I'd like that. If you're half as accurate with a dart as you are with that needle, you'll be brilliant at darts."

"And if I'm not?"

Ian shrugged. "Doesn't matter. I'll still be happy that we're a team and at least you'll speak to me. That Darren never said a word."

Paula leant across him and picked up the remote. She switched off the TV, then took Ian's hand and stood up. "Come on, let's start team-building right now."

19. Kissing Cousins

Georgina gave a deep, happy sigh as she looked around. Everything was so perfect, so romantic. The ruins of the castle and wildflower studded grounds would have looked good under normal conditions she was sure, but in the early morning sun and all decked out ready for the wedding it was fantastic.

She had thought it a shame she wasn't going to be a bridesmaid, but changed her mind. There was no pressure on her, she could just relax and enjoy the day. Georgina watched as people scurried about putting the final touches together. White and silver flags, in all manner of old fashioned shapes fluttered in the light breeze. Rows of chairs stood ready, each draped in white gauzy fabric and finished with an enormous silver bow. At the end of each row was placed a tub in which grew a standard rose. White of course, with silver ribbons spiralled up the stems. An arch, decorated in greenery and more white flowers marked where the bride and groom would say their vows.

Georgina turned back towards the adjacent hotel, where she and the other guests were staying and saw she wasn't alone. The young man was dressed in jeans and a thin sweater but otherwise seemed perfect for the location. She could imagine him as an actor waiting to change into the costume of a gallant knight in search of a lady. Actually he'd look just as good in a morning suit ready to play the part of a groom but that idea didn't appeal to her nearly as much. She'd far prefer him to still be searching for his love. Probably he was, he only looked a few years older than her seventeen years.

"Perfect setting, isn't it?" he asked. He had a deep voice, the sort that could make the reading of a bus timetable worth listening to.

"Lovely. I almost expect the ghost of King Arthur to ride over that hill there and come galloping in."

"It's not quite that old. Richard the Lionheart is more likely. I'm Frederick by the way," he extended a hand.

"Georgina."

"Georgina Rutledge?" He kept her hand in his.

"That's right. I'm a cousin of the bride."

"And of mine, I believe."

"You're Freddie?"

"Guilty."

She didn't really remember him, but her mother had told her how she and her cousin had played together as children and how sweet they'd looked together. Sweet wasn't how she'd describe him now, exactly, but he had the kind of good looks which might have seemed that way once. Georgina herself still had the mass of strawberry blonde curls which had earned her that description.

"Why guilty? Were you mean to me?"

"Teased you a fair bit, I think. You were so much younger than me and everyone made such a fuss of you I couldn't resist."

"You called me Rapunzel! I remember that."

"Sorry."

"Actually I… " Her phone buzzed before she could say she'd been delighted to be compared with a fairytale heroine. "Excuse me." It was a text from Mum wanting to know where she was. "I have to go. See you at the wedding?"

"Looking forward to it."

So was she, now more than ever.

As she got ready, she asked her mum about Freddie. "Are we really cousins?"

"Distant ones. What's known as kissing cousins, I think."

Georgina liked the sound of that.

She liked the wedding too. More than liked. It was everything she'd hoped it would be. Everyone looked fabulous, the weather was perfect, as was the moving ceremony. Afterwards Georgina sipped champagne and ate food so delicious her chef of a mother couldn't fault it. The cake, shaped just like the castle, only in white and silver not yellow stone, was exquisite.

There were real musicians, practically half an orchestra, who played traditional music during the wedding and later the kind you could actually dance to. OK so she didn't catch the bride's bouquet, but she did get to dance with Frederick and he did ask for her phone number and say they must keep in touch.

Reality didn't creep in until the following day. It started off with his parents and brother driving away early, in an expensive looking car, leaving Frederick to enjoy a more leisurely breakfast with Georgina and her mum. Then he explained he wasn't travelling with his parents as he was catching a train straight back to university. He was studying for a history degree in Exeter.

Georgina, feeling inadequate and dismayed at the distance between them, said she was retaking her GCSEs in Newcastle. Frederick didn't seem worried though and even kissed her cheek before getting on his train. He sent her a text twenty minutes later to check the one she and Mum were waiting for arrived on time.

"How come we never see Freddie and his family now?" she asked Mum.

"Oh I don't know. We used to live nearby and they'd have you round to play in their big garden while I was at work. Then we moved and you went to school. And we didn't have much in common really."

Still didn't, Georgina realised. Freddie, she supposed, came from the part of the family who got married in castles. She was the daughter of a single parent and lived in a council flat.

"They're snobs you mean?"

"No, I wouldn't say that. They were always very kind, but I didn't like to take advantage."

Georgina learned that some of her clothes had been hand-me-downs from Freddie's family. That most likely meant they'd once been worn by him. She smiled as she remembered him putting his jacket around her shoulders when they'd slipped out of the hotel to look at the castle in the moonlight. Had he realised that wasn't the first time his clothing had kept her warm?

Freddie phoned her and said he was trying to trace their family tree. "It's odd, everyone I've talked to is sure we're related, but no one seems to know how. Thought it'd be interesting for us to see how far back we need to go to find the link."

"Sounds fun. I'll ask around." She liked that he seemed to think she could offer something to the project and it would probably keep them in touch for some time. They emailed regularly and chatted via Skype exchanging any names or other information they discovered. Frederick found out far more than she did, but then he had more people to ask and was clearly better at research than she was.

The names Frederick and Georgina appeared frequently amongst both their ancestors. "It's common for names to be passed down through families," he explained, "so that does hint at a connection."

Just over a year after the wedding, Georgina and her mother received an invitation to spend two weeks in France with Frederick's family.

"We've hired a gîte that's more than big enough for us all to stay in and our son will be going almost right past you on the way to the ferry," Frederick's mum said. She tactfully explained the proposed arrangements, making it clear Georgina and her mum weren't expected to contribute financially.

"Can we go, Mum? Please."

"I don't like to impose."

"We're not. They asked us not the other way round. We could help with the cooking and washing up and things to make it fair." She got her way eventually. Putting on a Cinderella act in France would be better than not going anywhere, especially as it didn't seem there would be any sisters, ugly or otherwise, competing for the handsome prince's attention.

Of course it wasn't Freddie but his brother who took them over on the ferry, but Georgina still enjoyed the trip. She had been on a ferry a couple of times before, but she hadn't been about to spend two weeks in the south of France with… well with a very distant cousin she rather liked.

The gîte turned out to be a wonderful old farmhouse, with a huge kitchen range and racks of copper pans hanging from the ceiling. On the windowsills were pots of lush herbs and the cupboards and fridge were well stocked. Mum practically insisted she be allowed to cook. Georgina had been rather less forceful in her offer to do the washing up and not at all disappointed to learn one of the wooden doors hid a dishwasher.

Georgina and Frederick spent every day together. They walked for miles around historically interesting sites. The battles that had taken place, or people who'd lived there meant little to Georgina, but that didn't matter. The views were lovely and the company even better. She didn't need to understand everything Freddie told her to be caught up in his enthusiasm. When they stopped to rest he'd tell her about his progress on the family tree and gently apply suntan lotion to her shoulders.

"You go careful," Georgina's Mum warned her.

"We're not doing anything wrong."

"I didn't mean that. I don't want you hurt, that's all. He's from a rich family and obviously an ambitious man and you've only just left school... He likes you, love, but not the way you like him."

"He's only a few years older than me," Georgina said, although she knew that wasn't really what worried her mum.

In the evenings Freddie and Georgina sat in the garden and talked for hours. Pushing her concerns about their differences aside she was soon teasing him about being stuck in the past half the time.

"You belong in a history book."

"And you should be the beautiful princess in a fairy tale. In fact you're halfway there. You're beautiful, Georgina." He kissed her then.

It should have been perfect. The evening air was warm and scented with jasmine. Above them stars twinkled in the clear sky. But Frederick didn't pull her into his arms and give her the kind of lingering kiss that told her they'd be together always. When he put his hands on her shoulders and bent his head she'd been sure he was going to, but all he'd done was kiss the end of her nose and start talking about how red hair had once been considered a sign of royalty. That this was something to do with Henry the Eighth was the only detail that filtered through her disappointment.

Frederick liked her, she knew that, but it seemed his affection was still the kind they'd shared as toddlers. She told herself that was better than nothing and made the most of the rest of the holiday. Sleeping Beauty had waited a hundred years for a kiss and while she wasn't as patient as that, she saw it was no good trying to push Freddie. He often held her hand as they crossed rough ground or climbed steep steps. He hugged her when he made an exciting discovery. It was amazing how often he was thrilled by the details on a faded sign written in French, or the pattern of a few very battered tiles on the ground, but Georgina didn't mind in the least.

As she stood on the deck of the ferry watching France get smaller and smaller, Georgina told herself that what they'd shared was better than a holiday romance. Wonderful as that would have been, it would be over now. Their relationship was just beginning. The possibility that he simply wasn't at all romantically interested in her she attempted to dismiss entirely. Frederick was right, inside her head she did live in a fairy tale. Reality might have to be faced one day, but not yet.

Georgina printed out a few of her holiday pictures and took them to show her gran. The old lady was having a good day and recognised Georgina immediately. She did seem surprised at how much she'd grown, but then such a reaction is common in elderly relations. Over tea and cakes, they looked through almost a dozen picture albums, with Gran explaining who everyone was. Her memory of the past was quite vivid and Georgina took notes, sure some of the information would be of interest to Frederick. She borrowed a few photos too, so she could scan them and email the images to him.

Over the months, Frederick kept in regular contact by phone and email. He always seemed as interested in her news as in his own and the progress he was making on the family tree. He occasionally mentioned a girl, but it seemed his other relationships were no more serious than her own flirtations with boys she sometimes met.

He rang her one evening and excitedly said, "I think I've found it! My great-great-great-uncle referred to a man as his cousin. It's a legal document so it gives full names and it's exactly the same as your great-great-grandfather; Frederick Antony Augustus Harrington Rutledge. The man lives where he did and has the same occupation, so I don't think there's much doubt he really is your ancestor."

"That proves it then."

"Not exactly. It proves they thought they were related, not that they actually were."

"Oh, I see." She didn't really, as clearly there was a connection between them, just as there was a connection between her and Frederick. She could feel it, what did absolute proof matter?

Soon afterwards he started sending her love letters. Unfortunately not ones written to her. They were scans of part of a historical collection he'd learned about.

"I knew they'd appeal to you," he said. He knew her so well.

Although it was possible, likely even, the letters weren't necessarily written by members of their family. Such messages aren't generally signed with full names, nor supplied with precise dates and locations. There were hints though about historical events. In one the girl hoped she'd catch a glimpse of the King, though she knew he'd not be as handsome as her darling Nathaniel. In another a man mentioned his excitement that the 'Puffing Billy' was coming to Darlington.

"That's a train, isn't it?" she asked Freddie.

"It is. Don't tell me I'm winning you over to the cause of facts?"

"Absolutely not! I was imagining it steaming through a picturesque valley, taking a man wounded in the war back home and his fiancée eager to nurse him, but him being too proud to marry her now."

"But of course they will marry in the end and live happily ever after?"

"Absolutely."

The next time he rang, over two years after they'd been reunited at the wedding, Freddie suggested they go to a stately home together. Georgina agreed eagerly, then realised he hadn't even explained why.

"Did your great-great-great-great-great-grandad own it?"

"No, but I think your great grandmother's mother-in-law worked there. Actually I know she did and the servants' quarters are open to visitors."

"Oh, it's just lovely!" Georgina said when she saw the house.

"Pretty smart and from what I've read it's been really well restored. We should be able to see plenty of things your relative touched and cleaned. She was here a few years and got promoted a couple of times, so she probably went all over the house."

"You've really researched all this, haven't you? Is it part of your degree?"

"No, not precisely."

"Doesn't sound like you. Thought you were always precise."

"I can dream a little too, can't I? It's probably a family trait."

They looked round the grounds first as Georgina wanted to get a feel for the place before seeing where her ancestor had lived and worked. She also wanted to make the visit last as long as possible. Having Frederick by her side was much nicer than talking by phone, or even Skype.

"I can just imagine her walking along here, picking flowers for her room," she said as they walked around an ornamental lake. "Would they have been the same flowers?"

"Yes, I think the gardens have been restored to how they'd have been around the time she was here. I doubt she'd have been allowed to pick them though, or gone for walks in the little free time she got. Life was pretty tough below stairs."

"I suppose you're right… but maybe the lady of the house asked her to pick some, or perhaps the under gardener had a crush on her and gave her a bloom?"

He laughed. "Yes, OK that just might have happened. Perhaps they even managed to sneak out into the arbour amore together?"

"What's that? It sounds romantic."

"Oh it's right up your street. Legend has it that a couple who kiss in there will be together always."

"We're going to see it, right?"

"Absolutely." He took her hand and led her through a gap in the shrubbery. They stepped out into a small clearing, at the centre of which stood a small domed structure.

Once inside, Georgina kissed Freddie's cheek.

"Well that might be how the daughter of the house would kiss," Freddie said, "but I'm betting the scullery maid who's barred from having followers and the under gardener who risked his job by coming in here when he should be forcing rhubarb would do it more like this… "

His demonstration certainly seemed worth getting turned out of a job without a character reference for. When she could speak again, Georgina said, "If you pay that much attention to every aspect of your studies there's no doubt your degree will be a first."

"You know I like to do things properly."

"I do now."

Georgina enjoyed the rest of the day, but the facts had to fight for space in her head with the fairy tale playing out there. No way could he have kissed her like that if it didn't mean something. The kiss wasn't repeated though. He did kiss her again and hugged her tightly when they said goodbye, but it was much more of a cousinly kind of kiss.

"Talk soon," he said as she got on her train.

She thought of him, and his kiss all the way home. That night she remembered him saying her romantic nature was possibly a family trait. Maybe it was and that, plus the location and his love of history were what prompted the kiss. Sticking to facts like he did wasn't something Georgina usually did, but she tried to look at the truth of their relationship, uncoloured by her hopes.

The truth was that although he enjoyed her company, was kind and affectionate, he'd never once said he loved her. Mum was right, he just didn't feel about her as she did about him. Her role, in her own fairy tale, was that of unrequited love; pure, beautiful and tragic. Whenever they spoke or met again Georgina had great sympathy for her ancestor who'd made the most of any stolen moment from scrubbing and polishing to be with the man she loved, but who could never be hers. The sympathy was even greater when she started work at the only job she could get, assistant at the restaurant where her mother was once a chef.

Frederick got his degree, a first as she'd predicted. "Come out with me to celebrate? The result is partly thanks to you."

Over dinner he told her how trying to trace a link in their family trees had been the perfect leisure activity. The techniques he learned doing that assisted his studies and vice versa. "And our shared project helped prevent me having the sort of social life that would have been disruptive."

"No distracting girlfriends, just hours on the computer talking to me?"

"Something like that."

"Shame we never found the link."

"Don't give up so easily, Georgina. I'm not going to."

"I get the feeling you're not only talking about genealogy."

"I'm not." He reached across the table and took her hand. "Facts and figures don't mean much on their own. It's what they represent that matters. Those lives and people's hopes and dreams… I'm not putting it very well. It's like Anne Boleyn. I can tell you that she married Henry the Eighth on the twenty-fifth of February 1533, but that doesn't show his infatuation for her, how she meant so much to him he changed the religion of the whole country."

"And cut off her head?"

"OK, bad example. But it does show there's more going on than bare facts show. Take us, no proof we're related and technically we don't have much in common, but that doesn't mean… well, look at us."

She looked down at her hand in his.

"Fairy tales can come true, Georgina. Like… umm Hansel and Gretel? That is the one where they outwit the witch and live happily ever after in a house in the woods and live off shortbread?"

"That's the one," Georgina said. It was also the one where the hero and heroine were brother and sister. A close and loving couple, but not in any way romantic. She couldn't hide her sadness. "I think I understand. We shouldn't give up on our dreams, but they should be based on reality."

"That's it exactly." He seemed quiet after that. He must have realised he'd hurt her and was unhappy to have done so.

She didn't hear from him for a week. When she did he told her he had possible proof of their connection. "Can I come and show you?"

"Yes, of course."

Frederick gave her a photocopy of what looked as though it must have been a fragile document.

'Dear darling Georgina,

It feels as though I've loved you forever. So long in fact that I've not known a time when I didn't. Perhaps that's why it took so long to recognise my feelings, they're as natural to me as breathing.

Maybe I have indeed loved you forever. People say time is circular, that our past is our future and vice versa. I think that might be true.

I love you, Georgina. I want to be your past, your present and your future, just as I feel you are mine.

Marry me, my beloved,

Your devoted Frederick.'

"That's lovely! She did say yes, didn't she? And that's how we're related?"

"I don't know."

"I thought you said it was proof."

"Possible proof. If she says yes and marries him then it is how we're related."

"We can find that out can't we? Do you know when and where it was written?"

He nodded. "It was written quite near here."

"Then we can check the parish records, can't we? You know how to do that."

"Yes, but it won't be in there yet."

"Yet? I don't understand. When was this written?"

"Yesterday."

Georgina stared at him for a moment. "By you? To me?"

He answered with a kiss. And the rest is history, or a fairy tale, or both.

20. Three For A Girl

There wasn't really room for pacing up and down in the small caravan, but Maureen was doing her best. Impatiently she glanced out of every window, but the pretty view of green trees and blue skies did nothing to soothe her frazzled nerves.

About an hour previously she'd spotted a single magpie. One for sorrow. Try as she might, she couldn't see the second that would bring joy or the third or fourth that would indicate a girl or a boy. Maureen crossed over to where she'd seen the first one and caught a glimpse of smart black and white plumage. Was that it still there or another one?

"Come and sit down, love. You're wearing the carpet away. This is supposed to be a relaxing break for us," her husband, Arthur, said.

"I can't help it, I'm worried."

"What have you got to be worried about? Polly is in the hospital, with her husband and she's being well looked after."

"Yes, but… "

"She's only having a baby, not ill. That's what you used to say when you were expecting her."

"I suppose you're right."

"Put the kettle on then. A nice cup of tea might help calm us down."

"Us?" Maureen asked as she took the few steps to the two-ringed hob and lifted the small aluminium kettle.

"She's my daughter too, I'll be worried if I like."

"Oh, Arthur, I hadn't thought of you being worried, love." She put down the kettle and hugged him. "Sorry."

"I was kidding; I'm sure she'll be fine. Now, are you going to make that tea?"

"Yes, but it's no good getting impatient. You know it'll take ages to boil," she said as she filled the kettle and lit the gas.

"Me impatient!"

"What do you mean?" Maureen turned to face him; the battery powered lighter still in her hand.

"Ummm. That you're right. It will take a while, but I reckon we've got plenty of time. First babies always take ages don't they?"

As he spoke, Maureen saw her reflection in the mirror on the wardrobe door. She looked quite alarming brandishing the lighter and looming over poor Arthur in the confined space.

"Well, yes that's true," she answered gently. "Usually anyway."

Maureen set out the mugs, dropped in teabags and took the milk from the tiny fridge. She hunted through the overhead cupboards in search of custard creams.

"Arthur, do you think we should go back to the hospital once we've drunk this?"

"No, I don't. We were sent back here for good reasons. There's nothing we can do and this is supposed to be a holiday for us."

"Not exactly. You know I wanted to be near Polly when she had the baby."

"Yes, and that you wanted to be in the caravan so as not to

give her extra work."

"What's wrong with that? You said you didn't mind as it would be a sort of extra holiday."

"Exactly, so we should be relaxing and letting Polly and Mike relax too. You doing your impression of a coiled spring was making Polly nervous."

"Oh no! Do you think I've made things worse or brought bad luck or… "

"Calm down woman!"

The shriek from the kettle's whistle drowned out any reply Maureen might have been tempted to make. As she poured boiling water in the mugs, Arthur picked up his vibrating mobile phone.

"You had that on silent! We might have missed a call," Maureen said as he answered it.

"Fantastic… She has?" Arthur said into the phone.

"Who is it?" Maureen asked.

Arthur put a finger to his lips and Maureen realised that if she'd kept quiet when he answered she'd now know who was talking.

"Oh, Mike that's wonderful… really? What does that mean? … I've never heard of it… " He had to dodge about to stop Maureen snatching the phone out of his hand. "Oh, I see… good… really? Maureen will be pleased." He laughed. "Will do, see you soon."

"What is it? What's happened?"

"Mrs Cooper, you're a grandmother!" He hugged his wife. "Polly and her new daughter are just fine and we can go and visit whenever we like."

"Now?"

"Drink your tea first."

"What's the thing you'd never heard of?" Maureen asked as she took a sip of tea.

"A caul. It's very lucky apparently."

"Good, but what on earth is it?"

"It's part of the sac the baby's carried in, so Mike said. Sometimes it comes out covering the head. And is considered a lucky omen."

"How odd."

"It's quite natural… "

"I meant the omen thing. Some people have very strange ideas."

"Yes they do. Are you ready?"

Maureen grabbed her bag and stepped outside. Arthur locked the caravan door.

"Arthur, look quick! Three magpies."

21. Talk To Me

Alan listened to his daughter's giggles as she and her friends read their magazines. Chloe took advice from them, both the magazine columnists and her friends. He sighed. Why couldn't she ask him? OK, so his own freelance journalism on psychology wasn't generally aimed at teenage girls, but he's the one who knows her best, loves her best. Chloe gossiped on the phone for hours about nothing at all to her friends but she hardly talked to him.

Something was bothering her, he could tell, but he didn't know what. She'd started wearing thick black eye make-up. What was she trying to hide? She was so beautiful without it, just like her mother had been. Why did she want to make herself look cheap and ugly with all that stuff?

The girls all trooped out to go shopping and Alan considered going into Chloe's room and reading her diary. He did actually go in. His intention, he told himself, wasn't to read her diary, just to see if he could get a feel for what could be worrying Chloe. He saw a magazine abandoned open on the bed. He glanced through the article, by Becky Booker, about first dates. It gave good advice and Alan hoped his daughter and her friends would remember the suggestion to let their parents know where they were going, to meet their date in a public place and take a phone, make arrangements about how to get home and stick to them. To not be pressurised into anything they weren't ready for.

Alan pulled open a drawer to look for the diary. It was full of Chloe's underwear. He couldn't do it. Putting her clothes in the washing machine was one thing, rummaging through her underwear drawer was quite another. He couldn't read her diary either. That would be an even bigger invasion of her privacy and betrayal of her trust. Once she'd asked for a lock on her door. Alan remembered his response.

"You don't need one; I won't go in unless invited."

He put the magazine back where he'd found it and went downstairs.

Chloe had started wearing long gloves. Why? Was it a fashion statement, or could she be harming herself? Some girls did, he knew from his work as a psychologist. Surely his Chloe couldn't be doing that? Maybe his job made him worry too much. It certainly didn't help him to deal with his daughter. Sometimes he felt a complete fraud. In his newspaper articles he frequently advised others about communication, but he couldn't even talk to the child he adored.

Alan had tried talking to Chloe. When he gave her the good news that he'd been given a temporary slot with a popular magazine she'd just rolled her eyes and he'd not bothered giving her the details. It was a relief in a way she'd not asked any questions; the job was a touch embarrassing. Chloe did show a little more enthusiasm when he pointed out extra work meant extra money and he might be able to afford the pizza place for her birthday party after all.

"Awesome, Dad," she'd said and actually smiled.

Usually he just got a grunt or, if he was really lucky, a one word answer.

"Where are you going?" Had been his attempt yesterday evening.

"Out."

"Who with?

"Friends"

"Anyone I know?"

A shrug.

"Well, when will you be back?"

"Later."

"At what time?"

"I have to be in by ten, don't I? I have to look like a little kid running back home before I turn into a pumpkin while everyone else is out having fun."

He knew it wouldn't help to tell her that, to him, at fifteen she still seemed a kid half the time and for the other half she was a completely strange adult. He wished she was still a little kid. She'd loved him then and of course they'd still got her mother.

"I like your gloves," he tried, the next time Chloe was about to go out for the evening.

"Really?" She sounded a bit wary, but at least she was engaging with him. That was good wasn't it; or should he be worried the mention of gloves made her nervous. She wasn't being bullied at school was she? Maybe the gloves were to hide bruises?

"They look nice and warm." Stupid thing to say. They were lace, so didn't look particularly warm and in any case, Chloe wouldn't be wearing gloves for such a simple common-sense reason as to keep her hands warm.

"Daaad."

He'd deserved the mocking tone in her voice there.

Not drugs surely, she couldn't be injecting drugs into herself? No, he'd have noticed something. Surely he'd have noticed something.

"Well, have a nice time."

"Thanks. Oh, do you want me to post that?"

For a moment he was so stunned that she'd actually spoken a whole sentence he couldn't take in her meaning. Then he saw a letter he'd left on the hallway table.

"Thank you, that's very thoughtful of you."

"No bother, posting one for myself anyway." She held up an envelope.

He only caught a glimpse of it, but that was enough for him to recognise the name. He felt sick.

He couldn't take the letters off her and say he'd post them himself. She'd offered to do something for him, that was a real breakthrough. Having her do that was so important to her self-esteem. He couldn't make it seem he didn't trust her to do it properly and that his letter wouldn't arrive and he couldn't possibly explain that he didn't want hers to.

A couple of days later she burst into the kitchen and confronted him. "You go on about me not telling you anything, but you didn't tell me about your girlfriend."

"I don't have a girlfriend."

"Oh yeah? How come there's women's clothes in your wardrobe?"

"You've been going through my bedroom?"

"Don't change the subject!" She was nearly hysterical now. "Do you wear them yourself then, when I'm at school?"

"Don't be stupid, Chloe. For one thing, they're half my size."

"Why have you got them, then?"

"They were your mother's. I kept a few of her favourite things."

"Oh, Dad I… " The anger drained from her.

"I don't know why really. I sort of told myself you might like to have them one day, but really I just couldn't bring myself to throw everything away. I didn't want to open the wardrobe door in the mornings and see her side empty… "

Chloe put her arms round him and hugged. "I'm so sorry, Dad."

"It's OK, love."

"I miss her too. I know you think I don't, but I do. I remember her singing to me and stroking my hair. She did it just like you do."

Of course he did it the same way. After her mother died, Chloe wouldn't sleep. He tried everything to soothe her. The only thing that worked was to gently stroke her hair, just as he'd seen his wife do. It had comforted them both. By carrying out the same action he felt close to her and maybe it helped Chloe feel she hadn't lost everything.

That was the only trace of his wife that remained, apart from the dress she'd worn as the going away outfit at their wedding and the one she'd been in the day she'd told him she was pregnant and a couple of others associated with happy memories. He hadn't wanted to keep anything she'd worn or even touched when she'd been so ill those last few months. The photos had all been put away because seeing them had made Chloe cry and cry for the mother who'd gone forever.

"I shouldn't have gone into your room, Dad. I'm sorry."

"Why did you?" he asked as gently as he could.

"I was looking for a picture of Mum."

"I've got some. Come on, I'll show you."

They both cried as they sat on his bed and looked through the album. They hugged too. There were wedding photos and ones of her pregnant and one of her and Chloe on her first day at school. She'd been ill then, but it hadn't shown too much and the pain was eclipsed by her huge smile and pride in her daughter.

"I don't even remember that, Dad. She walked me to school and I don't remember."

"It's OK, I do."

He'd followed in the car to pick her up again. She hadn't been strong enough to walk both ways, but she'd insisted she walk Chloe to school just once.

"I remember you taking me."

"You do?"

"Yes. I think that helped me get lots of friends. All the yummy mummies wanted to talk to you so I was introduced to all the kids."

"Yummy mummies, eh? Maybe I should start walking you to school again?"

"Don't you dare!" she was only pretending the outrage. "Anyway, there's no point. No one's mum walks them to school now."

"I suppose you're right… Chloe, you remember we talked about trust?"

"Yes, Dad. I know I shouldn't have gone into your room. I was already feeling a bit guilty when I opened your wardrobe. I think that's why I reacted so badly, I wanted it to be you, not me, in the wrong."

He felt so proud of her self-analysis there. Maybe wanting to look inside people, to understand them, was something they shared.

"I won't do it again, I'm sorry. Is there anything I can do to make it up to you?"

For a minute he was tempted. 'Tell me about the gloves' he could insist, or 'Tell me what's on your mind'. That wouldn't be fair though.

"Well, I expect the fright you got is punishment enough."

There was still a way he could find out. He had to get rid of that temptation before he gave into it. He showed her the envelope she'd posted on the day she also posted one for him.

"How did you get that?"

"You were sort of right about there being another woman in my life. It's Becky Booker."

"But she's only twenty!"

"Actually, she's nearly thirty and pregnant, er, and forty-three and male."

"That makes no sense, Dad."

"It does in publishing terms. Becky Booker is more than one person. The photo on the column isn't of the regular writer, but as I said she's pregnant. She's had trouble with her blood pressure so someone else is standing in."

Chloe looked about to cry again. "It's your baby?"

"No, love. Being Becky Booker is my temporary job. Remember I told you about it?"

"But… I didn't really listen, did I?"

"No. I didn't really explain very well either. I was embarrassed about it and we need the money so I didn't want you to try talking me out of it." He gave her the envelope.

"It's still sealed."

"I saw who your letter was addressed to so I checked every envelope until I recognised your handwriting."

"But you didn't read it?"

"No. I want very much to know what's been worrying you and to help if I can, but I need you to trust me for that to happen."

"Read it."

"Only if you're sure."

Chloe nodded.

'Dear Becky Booker,

I can't seem to communicate with my dad. I think it's because my mum is dead and I look like her. There aren't any pictures of her anywhere, but I know I do because Gran told me. I try hard to look different by wearing lots of make-up and different clothes, but it doesn't help. I even wear gloves so he can't see my hands because I bite my nails just like she did. He told me once it was her only fault. I've got lots of faults. I bet he wishes I'd died and not her.

How can I make my dad love me?'

It was a good thing he knew who'd written it because his tears had obliterated the signature.

"You don't need to answer it, Dad. I already know you love me."

Twenty minutes later she was getting ready to go out again, but she did tell him where she was going and who with.

"We'll be back by ten and I've got my phone with me." She blew him a kiss and left.

Alan went into the kitchen to make tea and found a note by the kettle.

'Dear Becky Booker,

Got any tips for getting Dad to put up my pocket money?'

22. A Proper Holiday

"I'd like to have a proper holiday, just once," I told Staff Nurse Linda Baines.

"Well you deserve it, Julia. You're the hardest working porter this hospital has. But I thought you were all going to Lanzarote next week?"

"We are. Self-catering. By the time I've packed for all five of us, organised tickets, passports, cooked and cleaned for the whole fortnight, entertained the kids, then unpacked and done all the washing when we've got back I'm exhausted."

"You're not looking forward to it then?"

"I am really, it's just not my idea of a real holiday. I even do all the driving because Tim likes to take a complete rest from all responsibility."

"Can't you get him to help out a bit?"

"It's not that easy. He doesn't realise how much work a holiday is for me. It's my own fault really. I should have told him and refused to book self-catering. The kids can be difficult about unfamiliar food though. I feel better now I've got it off my chest. Sorry about the moan."

"Don't worry Julia, that's what friends are for. Sorry, but I'd better get to the ward, my shift starts at three."

"And I'd better start packing."

"Don't forget the sunscreen."

"No, nurse. I won't," I assured Linda.

I wasn't going to make the mistake I'd made before. Previously I'd packed for Tim and the boys first and not left enough time for my own things. I'd ended up throwing in clothes at random and having nothing suitable or comfortable to wear. This time I tried things on first, to check they still fitted and didn't have broken zips or unstitched hems.

Once everything was neatly folded, I just managed to do up the suitcase. It was heavy, but I decided I should take it downstairs right away, or else I'd be forever opening it to check I hadn't forgotten anything. That was a mistake. I caught the strap around the banister and fell down the stairs.

For a few moments I just lay in a tangle; whimpering. I was sure I must have done some serious damage. I half crawled to the phone and pressed the auto dial number for my neighbours. Mrs Adams volunteered to collect the boys from school and look after them whilst her husband drove me to hospital. Linda spotted me the moment Mr Adams helped me over to the reception desk in casualty.

"The lengths some people will go to avoid a bit of packing. Couldn't you just have asked Tim to do it?" she joked.

There's a thought, he might have to do his and the boys' now.

Linda took me into a cubicle so I could be examined. After the X-ray, Mr Adams sat by my side as we waited for the result. He assured me he would stay until I was either admitted or he could take me home. Linda came in. She wasn't smiling or joking any longer.

"I'm sorry, Julia, your shoulder is dislocated. The doctor will be able to manipulate it back into place, but it's going to hurt."

When the doctor arrived, Mr Adams was asked to return to the waiting room. He went, but that didn't prevent him hearing my yelp of pain.

Linda secured my arm with strapping and a sling.

"You won't need to stay in hospital. There are no broken bones. You will have a lot of bruising and it will be very swollen for a day or two. He's prescribed some painkillers. I'll get them for you before you go."

"Thanks. Linda, can I still go on holiday, did he say?"

"Yes, you can go, but you must be very careful. You mustn't use that shoulder for at least three weeks. You can't carry anything, you certainly can't drive. I don't even want you picking up a cup of tea with that arm. Do you understand? That means no work at all, or you'll make it worse and end up in a hospital instead of a hotel."

Tim did the rest of the packing. His own, Martin's and Justin's weren't too much trouble, I sat on the bed and gave advice. He had more trouble with Gavin, who insisted he couldn't possibly go without Big Ted. As the teddy would take up all the space in our largest case, that didn't leave room for clothes. I didn't let Tim fret for too long before I reminded Gavin that Big Ted gets very travel sick. I convinced him the bear would prefer to stay home and we'd send postcards.

I read the travel guide in the evening whilst Tim cooked tea. I made a note of some places I would like to visit. I may have been injured, but I didn't intend letting that spoil my holiday. Thanks to the painkillers, my shoulder now just felt slightly uncomfortable, rather than painful.

Linda arrived to see us off and helped Tim get the cases and boys into the car, ready for the drive to the airport. She handed me a note, which I read once we were on the motorway.

"What's so funny?" Tim asked.

"Linda has some last minute health advice. She says I must drink all my cocktails through a straw, so I don't have to lift them."

We got to the airport in plenty of time, which was just as well, because it took quite a while for Tim to struggle with the cases and children and repeatedly dropped bags, to the check-in desk. I felt sorry for him as I strolled behind with just my hand luggage. Tim realised that providing tickets and passports to the booking clerk might seem to be just a matter of organisation to those waiting impatiently behind him, but with a case in one hand and an excited child on the other arm it was not quite so simple. I got the distinct feeling he wouldn't be annoyed with me the next time I sorted frantically through my bag to locate the necessary documents.

I think Tim was pleased that he'd listened to my advice to pack crayons, comics, puzzle books and card games into the hand luggage. At the time, he'd not seen the benefit of lugging round the extra weight for a four-hour plane journey. As we watched other children running excitedly around the departure lounge, demanding sweets, toys and attention, we were grateful that our three were content with a few words of praise for their neat colouring in, and the reading of stories.

Almost nine hours after checking into Gatwick, we arrived at our accommodation. None of us wanted more than a bowl of soup for supper and to go to bed. The following morning was not so calm. The boys were up early and eager to explore. They were less than happy to learn they would have to wait until Tim had visited the hotel's small shop, before they could get up. They weren't pleased to learn, on his return, that there would be a further delay whilst everyone washed, ate breakfast and the clothes were unpacked before they could go out. They didn't want to use the strange bathroom alone, so Tim had to wash them. I noticed he hadn't shaved quite as smoothly as usual. Perhaps that's something he does better without assistance.

I heard the boys complaining about the cereal. They didn't recognise the packaging and so mistrusted the contents. I switched on the shower and didn't hear Tim's reaction. As I walked out of the bathroom, I smelt something delicious cooking. Tim had taken the boys back to the shop and he was serving up baked beans, bacon, fried eggs and mushrooms.

Once we'd eaten, I took the boys for a walk to look at the pool, and other facilities the hotel had to offer. I also checked the timetable for details of the journey to the beach. I kept the boys out as long as possible, to give Tim a chance to clear up from breakfast, unpack and prepare our picnic lunch. He hastily threw swimming gear, towels and suncream into a bag and we just caught the bus.

The boys raced off to select a suitable spot on the beach. When Tim and I reached them, I sank with a sigh onto a towel on the warm sand. Tim did the same, and then almost immediately had to get up to help the boys change into swimming trunks and cover them in protective lotion. He helped me to remove my sling and gently smoothed lotion onto my sore shoulder. I didn't intend going home with a large white patch as a reminder of my accident. I enjoyed seeing the children and Tim build sandcastles and race around in the surf. I sat up and watched them each time I reached the end of a chapter in my book. I was happy to stay on the beach as long as they wished, so we caught the last bus back.

Tim made a delicious tea of spaghetti Bolognese, followed

by fresh fruit salad and ice cream. I read the boys a story whilst he cleaned up from supper. I asked him to open a bottle of wine. I sipped a glassful as he put the children to bed. He poured himself a glass and joined me.

"Tim, I'm so glad you talked me into coming here. To think I wanted to go to Butlin's. I know it would have been easier, but this is much better."

"I expect Butlin's would have been OK. The kids would have enjoyed it."

"Yes, but they're enjoying it here too. Here we can be more independent," I reminded him of his reasons for choosing this type of holiday. "We can eat what we like when we like. We can enjoy ourselves as a family too, rather than have the kids missing half the day at some club."

I thought Tim was going to say something, but he just reached for his glass and gulped down some of the cool, crisp, wine.

The following morning I asked the kids to fetch the items we'd need for the day and put them in the beach bag as Tim washed up from breakfast.

"I'll need to go to the shop for more bread," he said.

"Yesterday I noticed a snack bar on the beach. Shall we have lunch there?"

"Oh that's a lovely idea," Tim replied.

I smiled at him and he looked thoughtful. I'm sure he remembered that I'd made exactly the same comment last year, when after ten days he had wondered if I might prefer not to prepare a meal for a change.

After he'd got the kids ready to play on the sand, he again helped me with my sling and smoothed on some cream.

"I'm sorry you've got to look after me as well as the boys.

I'm not being much help am I?"

"It's not your fault. Anyway, I think you've probably been more help than I've been to you on our other holidays. I'm sorry, I didn't realise that you never got a proper holiday. We'll do things differently in future."

"Let's start now. You don't have to cook all the time, we can eat out. It's a shame not to try the local food."

The rest of the holiday was beautifully relaxing. The weather was wonderful. We travelled everywhere by bus, so Tim and I were able to admire the scenery rather than concentrating on driving an unfamiliar car on foreign roads. There was almost no shopping, cooking or washing up as we ate out for every meal, except breakfast.

Tim and the boys slept for most of the late night flight home. I found Linda's note in the pocket of the jacket I'd not worn since the outward flight. I read it again. Funny thing, I'd read it so quickly the first time, I'd missed a few lines.

'I confess, I exaggerated the seriousness of the damage to your shoulder. You need to give it complete rest for three days – not weeks. I just wanted to get you out of all that packing, and show Tim that there's more work than he realises involved in a relaxing holiday. You can take the sling off as soon as you're ready.'

I smiled. Oh dear, it looked like Linda's plan had worked all too well. Then I remembered the cases full of grubby clothes and the school uniforms that needed ironing. I remembered too, that Tim had remarked only this morning how bruised my shoulder still was. Perhaps it would be best to keep the sling on for just a couple more days.

23. I Mean It This Time

Karen unplugged the iron and pulled on the warm blouse.

"Hurry up with your breakfast," she urged her daughter, Anna.

Karen gulped down her coffee, stacked the breakfast crockery in the dishwasher and switched off the television. As usual she'd missed hearing most of the news. Anna always chatted through it. Why couldn't the girl just eat her cereal?

"Hurry up, Anna, or you'll be late and your teacher will be very cross."

"I don't want to go to school today, Mummy," Anna said as Karen attempted to zip the girl's coat.

"You don't? But I thought you liked it. All the painting and story books and it's cooking today."

"I like that, but I don't like break-times. Nathan is horridable to me."

Karen didn't have time for schoolroom squabbles. Anna had to go to school and if Karen didn't take her right now, then she'd be late for work.

"Would you be able to keep away from him today, do you think?" Karen asked.

Anna nodded but didn't look convinced.

"If you go to school, you'll be making scones for our tea. What will we do without the scones?"

"OK, Mummy."

On the way to school, Karen got stuck in a worse than

usual version of the regular traffic jam.

"There's my friend," Anna informed her, pointing to a girl Karen recognised. She was walking with her mother.

"I don't blame them for walking, it's probably quicker," Karen muttered.

"Shall I walk with them, Mummy?" Anna asked.

Good idea, if Anna did that, Karen could take a more direct route to work. She pulled into a bus stop and hastily checked the arrangement was OK with the other girl's mother.

While waiting for a gap in the traffic, so she could rejoin the row of slow moving cars, Karen switched on the car stereo. Anna must have been fiddling with it again, because instead of a CD, Karen was listening to the news. Why hadn't she thought of that before? It would make more sense to hear it when driving than divide her attention between her daughter and the newsreader over breakfast. The report was about the increase in bullying at school and how much younger children were being affected. Karen shook her head. Surely teachers should have sorted this out by now?

Karen had been bullied herself and knew how awful it could be. She'd been picked on for having braces and glasses. Mum told her to ignore them. Most kids got bored with the teasing after a few days of getting no reaction, but one girl, Vicky, hadn't given up. She'd taken Karen's sweets saying she couldn't eat them with all that metal in her mouth and had scribbled in her books saying she was too blind to see what was there. Teachers tried to stop it, but that just moved the bullying outside the school gates. Vicky cycled ahead and jumped out on Karen as she walked to school or on her way home. Never knowing when or where the attacks might come from had made it worse.

An accident caused an end to the bullying. Vicky fell off her bike and ripped her school uniform. She'd cried and thinking she was badly hurt, Karen investigated.

"My dad will kill me," Vicky had wailed.

"Don't be silly," Karen replied. It made a change to see the bully upset and at a disadvantage for once. "Dads buy sweets and tell you stories if you're hurt."

She'd learnt that Vicky's dad wasn't like hers. Karen had taken Vicky home and persuaded her mum to repair the uniform.

"Vicky won't ever be nasty to me again if you mend it and no one tells her dad."

Karen had been tempted to tell people at school about Vicky's accident. They'd laugh at her falling off and showing her knickers and once they knew she was easy to scare she'd turn from bully to victim. Karen knew how awful that was. Instead she'd persuaded Vicky it would be better if no one got bullied and Vicky had promised to try to break up trouble instead of causing it.

Over breakfast, this morning, Anna had talked about someone getting knocked over and hurting themselves. Karen admitted to herself she hadn't really been listening. Getting Anna to school had seemed more important than what happened once she was there. Could it be that Anna was being bullied? She'd have to have a proper talk with her this evening and find out what, if anything, was going on.

The shortcut to work wasn't as quick as Karen had hoped, due to a broken down bus. To make matters worse, a traffic report on the radio mentioned the roadworks and Karen realised she'd heard it earlier and taken no notice. What was the point of having the radio on if she wasn't going to listen properly? She searched the glove box for a CD to cheer herself up. A car beeped, indicating the bus had moved and Karen was now the one causing the hold up. She put up a hand in apology and was rewarded by another blast on the horn.

Once at work, Karen was summoned to her boss's office.

"You've approached this report from totally the wrong angle. If you didn't understand what I wanted, why an earth didn't you ask?"

Once he'd explained again, Karen stomped off to redo the task that she'd already wasted three days on. It wasn't fair for her to be blamed for his poor explanation. She'd better get herself a coffee and calm down or she wouldn't be able to concentrate.

In the canteen, Karen overheard the transport manager's PA telling her friends about the cute things her kid said. Remembering the funny way Anna had described cauliflower as 'veg-de-bubble clouds' a few days ago, Karen joined in the conversation.

"She calls broccoli baby trees too," Karen said.

"My Nathan does the same thing," the PA said. "Maybe it's something they get from school. My little darling goes to St Mark's, what about your daughter?"

The woman was Nathan's mum!

Karen informed the woman that he might be a darling at home, but he wasn't quite so nice at school.

"My Nathan, are you sure?"

"Of course I'm sure. You don't think my six-year-old would lie about this, do you? Poor mite used to love school and now she dreads it."

"Well that's a pity, but I don't think you can blame my son. He's really a… "

"I can and I do. You ought to take a bit more notice of what your son gets up to. He'll turn into a right thug if you don't and… "

"How dare you come in here and lecture me on how to bring up my child! Yours is hardly a little angel if she takes after you," the woman shouted. She stormed out the canteen, crashing into Karen as she went.

It was easy to see where the boy got his rough behaviour from, Karen thought as she rubbed her arm. The woman hadn't been the slightest bit apologetic and had yelled at Karen instead of listening. If Nathan's mother wasn't going to deal with his bullying behaviour, then it was up to the school, or Karen herself, to take action.

She thought about the incident with Vicky, could something like that be arranged? Tempting though it was, she couldn't go around knocking small children off their bikes. There must be something she could do; surely a six-year-old wasn't too hardened in his bad habits to be reformed? First, she'd need to arrange time for a quiet chat with Anna to find out as much as the girl knew.

"How was school today?" Karen asked her daughter that evening. "Did Nathan bother you?"

"No, we played pirates, but the teachers were horridable."

"The teachers?"

"Yeah, they said I couldn't have my sweets at break time."

"Honey, you know you don't have sweets except at the weekends because they're bad for your teeth and why did you play with Nathan if he's nasty to you?"

"He's nice to me because his mummy is horridable too."

Karen had to agree that Nathan's mum was horrible, but she didn't understand who else was.

"You said you'd make all my teeth fall out and hurt if you gave me sweets, so Nathan shared his with me. I promised not to tell anyone he took his hat off, so his mummy wouldn't make him be ill."

"His mummy makes him ill? What do you mean?"

"She said if he doesn't wear his hat she's going to make him have a horridable cold."

"Oh dear, sweetheart. It's not me who'd make your teeth hurt or Nathan's mummy who'd make him ill."

She tried to explain why parents make rules and occasionally say things they don't mean. Maybe Anna wasn't the only person who misunderstood what she heard?

"Anna, love, when you told me that Nathan was nasty to you, what exactly did he do?"

"I told you, he ate all his sweets and didn't give me any just because I laughed when he fell over in a puddle and hurt his knee."

"He didn't hurt you or anything… ?"

"Course not, Mummy. Only bullies do that and the teachers told us it's very bad to be a bully because no one will like you and you'll be in trouble."

Karen was pleased to hear the school took bullying seriously and tried to prevent it. She was pleased too that Anna listened to her teachers. What a shame Karen hadn't listened so carefully to her daughter and remembered the lesson she'd learned as a child.

A few weeks after she'd fallen off her bike, Vicky had asked to be Karen's friend. Karen had agreed and after a few more weeks had passed, she'd gone to tea at Vicky's house. Vicky didn't have a mummy, just the evil daddy. He'd laid a table full of food for their tea and poured both girls a glass of milk. Karen had watched nervously as he picked up a big, sharp knife.

He must have noticed her staring as he said, "Would you like to cut the cake, Karen?"

Her hands had shaken and the knife seemed to have a mind of its own. Instead of slicing through the delicious looking chocolate cake, it had stabbed down onto the table, cutting the white lace cloth. Vicky yelped.

"Don't hurt me!" Karen had sobbed, if he'd been angry with Vicky for ripping her awful school uniform, what would he do to her for wrecking the lovely tablecloth?

"Of course, I won't," Vicky's dad said. He'd looked at his daughter's worried expression. "Oh girls, I'm sorry. I promise I have no intention of hurting either of you however much material you rip. It's just that it's hard to look after Vicky and the house all on my own and sometimes I say things I shouldn't."

After that, Karen's mother had washed and mended all of Vicky's clothes and helped her dad with other things too. Vicky had been much nicer and happier after that and Karen had learned that sometimes when grown-ups are cross they say things they don't mean.

She hugged Anna. "I promise I'll never hurt you, honey. Not even if you're really naughty and I get very cross."

"OK, Mummy. Can I have some sweets?"

"No you can't and you must stop asking Nathan for his."

"That's what he said. He's going to eat them when I'm not there."

"So you are friends now?"

"Yes."

Karen hoped it would be as simple for her to make friends

after falling out with Nathan's mum.

At work, Karen approached the woman she'd shouted at the day before. "I'm sorry about yesterday, really sorry."

"Me too. I guess we're both guilty of saying things we didn't mean?"

Karen held out a hand. "I'm Karen, is there any chance we could be friends?"

The woman shook her hand. "Ah yes, the toothrotting demon. I'm Suzy the flu virus, nice to meet you."

"It might be nice for our kids to see we're happy for them to be friends. Would you and Nathan like to come to my house for tea tomorrow?"

"I would. Maybe we could discuss a shared school run, too? I'm sure we could both use a bit more time in the mornings."

After Karen bought chocolate cakes (individual ones, so her knife could stay safely in the kitchen drawer) she rang Vicky.

"Hi, Vicky. I've been saying things I didn't mean and it made me think of you. We said we'd be friends forever and I did mean that, but I haven't kept in touch and I wanted to apologise."

"Don't apologise. I've been no better, but we'll sort it out. So come on then, tell me all your gossip."

24. Odd Socks

"Chill, Mum." That was from Eve, my nine-year-old.

"It was a joke," Simon said. He wasn't laughing but what kid does when his mum shouts at him when he's… taking the washing out the drier.

I breathed and tried to replay their voices. Eve mentioned an affair and Simon thought it funny. That's it, Eve said, "I reckon Mum's having an affair with a three legged man." Simon countered with, "Or three one legged men." See, I did listen to my kids, even if what they said made no sense.

"What's going on?" I demanded.

"It's all the odd socks," Eve said. She held up three.

Odd socks, right. Just a joke. Not funny, but at least they weren't siding with Tony against me. Good. Just as well, as it was because of them I was tense and irritable.

"Why are you messing about with them?"

"To put on our feet." Eve didn't actually say 'duh' but it was in her tone.

I felt guilty then; I haven't really been keeping up with that side of things. Who am I kidding? If Tony hadn't been doing practically all the housework these last few months the place would have been condemned as uninhabitable by now. I couldn't really begrudge him taking a morning off to play golf, but why did it have to be right then? I had enough on my plate without… Oh.

"Come on, breakfast. What do you want?" It better be toast with chocolate spread – I didn't have time for anything else. They did still like that, didn't they?

"Something that takes up so much room there won't be space for your laptop on the table," Eve said.

"Don't be silly, I… "

"You what? Wouldn't do that?"

Actually I was going to say I had to check my emails. Well I did.

"Well, Mum? Can you spare us ten minutes of your time?"

"Of course!" Of course I would, just not right then. I had to check those emails to see if the figures had come through yet. If not, I'd either be working through the night again, or kissing my promotion goodbye.

"The kitchen is that way." Even Simon was sounding sarcastic.

Once there I saw bowls washed on the draining board and that it was much later than I'd thought. Help, I was further behind with work than I'd realised.

"You did say you could spare us ten minutes," Eve pointed out.

"Yes, yes. Was there something other than breakfast you wanted?" Once I had that promotion I'd be able to afford whatever it was. True I was having to make sacrifices to get there, but it'd be worth it. They're my kids. I love them, I'd do anything for them.

"A mum."

"Don't be silly, you've got one!" I was getting a sense of deja vu. It was very like the previous night's conversation with Tony. He said he wanted a wife. Said I was never there, didn't care. How dare he! That's what I said, or probably shouted. He just muttered I should see things from someone else's point of view for once. Who did he think I was doing this for? True I was spending more time and money on my appearance, but you have to dress up to move up if you're a woman. True I didn't spend much time with the family, but once I had the new job we'd be able to afford nice holidays, spend a bit of quality time together.

He said he was going to golf the next day and leaving me with the kids. Maybe they'd make me see sense. Well that wasn't working, they were just distracting me from what I should be doing.

"We're going to give you a quiz to see if that's true," Simon said.

If what was true? Oh yes, them having a mum.

"Number one, what sport am I best at?"

"You're good at everything," I said.

"Two, the name of my best friend?" Eve asked.

"You have so may friends, it's hard to keep up."

"What was your favourite thing to do when you were a kid?"

"What?" Back then it was all so simple. There were actually more hours in the day, I'm sure of it. I spent weekends walking in the woods with my parents looking for wild flowers and birds. In spring we searched for the first primrose, summer we picked blackberries, autumn we tried to catch leaves as they fell and in winter...

"How much did it cost?" Eve interrupted my thoughts.

Money, it's all about money. And if they kept on wasting my time I wouldn't ever be able to earn enough. I stomped upstairs and opened my laptop. There was an email – from Tony.

'If you're reading this you couldn't answer the quiz questions.

1. Football. Simon is so good he's won a scholarship for a sport's academy.

2. Lisa. She has leukaemia. The iPod Eve wanted was for her.

3. Walking in the woods with your family. Do you remember telling me that?

4. Nothing. That's what it cost and that's what it will cost you to get this family back. Nothing but time. Meet me at twelve if you're prepared to spend some of that on us. If not, get back to work and good luck with the promotion. I know it's important to you. I just hope it's not more important than us.'

I scrolled through my inbox, but I wasn't concentrating on work. I was thinking about my kids. With my promotion I could buy Simon a new football kit and presents for Eve's friend. Without it I could cheer from the touchline, or drive Eve to the hospital and talk to her about her pain.

It took me a little while to get my thoughts in order, then I started typing.

I returned to the kitchen holding a bunch of assorted socks. "I've no idea where your dad put the matching ones, so we'll have to wear these if we want to meet him for a walk."

"And do we want to do that?" Simon asked.

"Yes love, we do."

Later I'd explain I'd emailed my boss to say I was no longer looking for promotion. First though we'd look for birds and trying to catch falling leaves.

25. Foxing The Issue

While we were waiting to go in, Duncan held me close so my tears soaked his shirt and told me about a fox he'd seen at work.

"It was there a few days ago. Looked like it had been hit by a car or something. I considered trying to get it to a vet but it ran off before I could get near it, let alone think about catching it. It was dragging a leg but still moved faster than I can."

"Poor thing. I hope it didn't suffer for long."

"Oh, it's not dead. I see it every morning and a few of us have started leaving behind any food we've got left. It's gone by morning so I suppose he eats it."

"And the leg?"

"Still dragging. I can't tell if it hurts him."

Then our names were called and I forgot all about the fox.

The test results were a relief in a way. It meant we needn't go through any fertility treatments, fill in more charts, keep saying, 'no, not yet' to our mothers. I kept telling myself all that, whenever I wasn't sobbing so hard I couldn't think at all.

Duncan was upset too, I know. He comforted me and continued to function normally but I knew he was disappointed. No more than that. In his way he too was grieving. We've been together since we were at school you see, and we've been thinking about the family we'd raise since we were children ourselves.

Plenty of people told us our relationship wouldn't last and I think we believed them until we realised, at twenty-five, that we'd been together more than half our lives. We got married the following year and those people who'd once said it wouldn't last started asking when we'd start a family. We laughed and said we'd hardly thought about it.

It wasn't true, we'd picked out names, lots of names. We were going to have eight children and give them so many names their initials spelled out words. We'd have all boys, or all girls. Half and half, twins, triplets. We'd refined our plans to just Emily and Jamie by the time we married. But that was our business. Something private. That's what we thought at first anyway.

As the months without any sign of a baby turned into years, it gradually seemed to be everybody's business. Not any more though.

After a time I got a grip on my grief. I don't mean it lessened, but I stopped crying all the time and began to give an impression of someone getting on with her life.

"I got another picture of him today," Duncan said one evening.

"Who?"

"The fox."

I'd been so wrapped up in my misery it took me a moment to understand what he was talking about. He'd probably been giving me regular updates on the poor creature but I'd not paid attention. It wasn't fair for Duncan to lose his wife as well as the children he'd hoped for.

"Show me."

The picture on his phone wasn't very clear as the fox was lurking in a shadow none too close, but I could see it was horribly thin.

"It's putting on weight though, I'm sure. Here look." He scrolled threw and showed me the first photo he'd taken. He was right, it had looked even worse before.

The next day I accepted the counselling I'd been offered. It helped a little. I was told about taking control of my situation. I couldn't change the fact that Duncan and I would never have a baby, but I could control some things about my future. I could consider fostering or adoption, I could decide to accept that we'd not have a family and decide to travel or… well, there were lots of options.

When I told Duncan he was delighted I was feeling more positive and beginning to look forward, but he didn't do what I'd done, and what I'd expected from him, and seize on one of those options as the obvious answer.

"Adoption is something to think about," I prompted.

"I believe it's quite complicated though and a lot of people don't get selected." He squeezed my hand. "We can look into it, if you like."

Maybe it seems odd that we'd not considered adopting, but you don't if you're so sure you'll have your own child and I had been sure for so long. I mean I had realised that some people get pregnant the minute they come off the pill and I hadn't and that most people get pregnant within a year of trying and I hadn't.

By two years Duncan and I had worked out there was a chance that something wasn't quite right but we just thought it was a delay, not a no.

I'd got on the internet and looked for things we could do. I learned the best time to conceive and about taking my temperature, hence the charts I no longer needed. We adopted a healthier diet, exercised more. Duncan got cool, roomy underwear. Oh and we did some weirder things too, we ate a lot of yams, took phases of the moon into account and I spent a lot of time lying with my feet in the air after… you know, afterwards.

It was fun at first and there was no hurry. We'd been happy just the two of us for sixteen years and we were still young. Another few months wouldn't matter. Of course none of it helped but that wasn't the fault of the world wide web, so I tried it again for my latest, far more minor problem; Duncan's fox. He'd told me it wasn't gaining any more weight.

"Everyone gives it scraps now and it's getting quite tame. I dropped the piece of pastry I was going to throw and he ran up and snatched it from right by my boot. And Dave, one of the lorry drivers, always brings him chips and Franz sits right under his cab window and catches them as they fall."

"Franz?"

"A bit more classy than Freddie, I thought."

And why not, we'd decided on Emily for our imaginary daughter because he considered it a classier version of the name of our favourite Spice Girl.

"So he's eating well but not getting any better?"

"I think the leg is improving a bit, but he doesn't look healthy."

After we'd eaten I looked up urban foxes on the internet. I read that a diet of scraps wasn't ideal for them. Obvious really when you think about it.

"I think Franz needs to start a healthy eating plan. Take him the mince that's in the fridge."

"The best steak mince you were going to make me spaghetti Bolognese with?"

"I can buy more tomorrow so you'll still get your spaghetti and you're worried about him, aren't you?"

"Suppose. Do you think I'm silly?"

"No. Caring that's what you are." That's one of the reasons he'd make such a good dad, but I didn't say so then.

I waved him off the following morning, with his box of salad and pack of raw mince. Then I did the chores, including buying some offcuts of meat for Franz before returning to the computer. I typed 'adoption' into the search engine.

It took the time needed for the first image of a woman with a baby in her arms to load for me to decide adoption was the answer. Several hours of searching later I was convinced we met all the criteria and had a good chance of adopting a baby and an even better chance if we agreed to take a slightly older child. That was my favoured option as it would make up for some of the time we'd lost. I downloaded all the information we'd need to start the process and waited for Duncan to come home.

"We can adopt," I blurted out before he'd got out the car. "I'm sure they'll accept us and I've got all the forms and everything."

"Whoa, calm down, love!"

"Sorry, I'm just excited."

"Yes, I can see that."

As he got washed and changed I told him some of the things my internet searches had revealed.

He towelled his hair and said, "We need to think about it, look into things."

"I have," I started to say but then stopped. I had rather sprung it on him and Duncan is the sort who likes to think things through before making a decision. You know, date a girl for twelve years before proposing, that kind of thing. I restrained my enthusiasm and tried to give him space by changing the subject.

"Did Franz enjoy his mince?"

"Seemed to. I sprinkled it over the grass so I could get another picture and he ate every scrap. Let me show you."

He'd taken several pictures of Franz and it was clear Duncan had got very close to the animal. It was clear too that Franz wasn't at all well. When I'd looked up urban foxes the day before I'd seen photos of some suffering from mange and he looked just the same. I flashed up the laptop to check the symptoms.

"Does he scratch himself?" I asked.

"Yes, he's always doing it."

"And you say he seems less frightened of you?"

"Yes. What are you looking at?"

He read the page. "Yeah, I'm pretty sure that's what's wrong. Click that link will you, the one for treatment."

We found that treatment was fairly simple if you could persuade the fox to swallow the medication and that he was likely to die slowly and painfully without it. There was no option, we ordered the cure and read up on how to administer it. Apparently hiding it in a jam sandwich was the recommended option.

"Well he's going to eat healthily until the stuff arrives," I said as I put all my printouts on adoption into a folder. I made sure my husband saw where I put it so he could look through when he was ready.

Duncan took meat to Franz for the rest of the week. We talked about the fox in detail and skirted around the subject of adoption.

"How can people give up a child?" he asked once.

"Lots of reasons," I said and gave a few examples.

"Would we know? If we took a child would we know why it had been abandoned."

"I don't know, but does it matter?"

"How can we care for them if we don't know? What would we tell them?"

"I don't know, love but we'd find a way. You don't know why there's a lame fox living in a car park to a construction project in the middle of a city but you're doing your best to help him."

"I suppose."

When Franz's treatment arrived Duncan took jam sandwiches and meat for a while. The results were incredible. Duncan said the scratching stopped very quickly and Franz soon looked more alert, more like a wild creature than a sick and injured pet. Soon I could see the difference in the photos. Every time Franz looked better though it got harder to tell as he no longer approached quite so close.

"I'm going to get some of these printed out," he told me. "Before and after kind of thing."

He did just that in his lunch break the following day. It was amazing to see the transformation Franz had gone through.

"Makes me feel quite proud to see what we've done."

"You did it," I told him.

"No, love. We did. We make a good team. I'll put these away now." He went to the drawer and took out my adoption file. "In here?"

Did that mean he was thinking he could show them to our adopted child one day?

"If there's room."

"There will be once we've sent these forms off."

It did. I cried again.

Duncan, still holding the photos of the fox, held me close.

Thank you for reading this book. I hope you enjoyed it. If you did, I'd really appreciate it if you could leave a short review on Amazon and/or Goodreads.

To learn more about my writing life, hear about new releases and get a free short story, sign up to my newsletter – https://mailchi.mp/677f65e1ee8f/sign-up or you can find the link on my website patsycollins.uk

More books by Patsy Collins

Novels –

Firestarter
Escape To The Country
A Year And A Day
Paint Me A Picture
Leave Nothing But Footprints

Non-fiction –

From Story Idea To Reader
(co-written with Rosemary J. Kind)

A Year Of Ideas:
365 sets of writing prompts and exercises

Short story collections –

Over The Garden Fence
Up The Garden Path
Through The Garden Gate
In The Garden Air

No Family Secrets
Can't Choose Your Family
Keep It In The Family
Family Feeling
Happy Families

All That Love Stuff
With Love And Kisses
Lots Of Love
Love Is The Answer

Slightly Spooky Stories I
Slightly Spooky Stories II
Slightly Spooky Stories III
Slightly Spooky Stories IV

Just A Job
Perfect Timing
A Way With Words
Dressed To Impress
Coffee & Cake
Not A Drop To Drink

Printed in Great Britain
by Amazon

25929645R00086